PENG

WUTHER

Bette Howell was born ir
Yorkshire. Her father was a miner and her mother a teacher. She served as a radar operator with an anti-aircraft battery in the war, for some of the time in Belgium. As a child she wrote stories and pantomimes to be acted out in the garden by a neighbourhood gang. Winning the *Mail on Sunday* Novel Competition in 1985 gave her the impetus to fulfil a lifelong ambition of becoming a full-time writer. Her second book, *Silver Riding*, continues the glorious adventures of May and Otley begun in *Wuthering Depths*. She now lives in Keighley, near Haworth.

BETTE HOWELL

Wuthering Depths

PENGUIN BOOKS

PENGUIN BOOKS

Published by the Penguin Group
27 Wrights Lane, London W8 5TZ, England
Viking Penguin Inc., 40 West 23rd Street, New York, New York 10010, USA
Penguin Books Australia Ltd, Ringwood, Victoria, Australia
Penguin Books Canada Ltd, 2801 John Street, Markham, Ontario, Canada L3R 1B4
Penguin Books (NZ) Ltd, 182–190 Wairau Road, Auckland 10, New Zealand

Penguin Books Ltd, Registered Offices: Harmondsworth, Middlesex, England

First published by Viking 1989
Published in Penguin Books 1990
1 3 5 7 9 10 8 6 4 2

Printed and bound in Great Britain by
Richard Clay Ltd, Bungay, Suffolk
Filmset in Baskerville

For
John and Richard Fabian

WE GOT out into the countryside like the doctor said. Otley dressed for Top Withens as for an assault on Everest: moleskin knickerbockers, map and compass round his neck and a yeti dangling from the back of his rucksack. I breathed the honey-scented air in ecstasy as our sandwiches curled up in the afternoon sun. Otley gave his to the sheep.

'I don't like shrimp paste,' he said. 'It's got eyes in; I saw some in a bag at Blackpool.'

I made sorry noises and secretly wondered if Brontëland was the right place for a nervous breakdown.

'Let's go back,' he said. 'I'm hungry.'

Otley felt safer indoors. He could sit in the attic and watch for the Russians coming then run down to the cellar and hide. He did strange things and we had long since forgotten the laughing boy who swam in the peaty waters of the tarn like a darting sunbeam. He went off to war a shining gold and came back with dark unfathomable depths.

'What happened over there?' I was once unwise enough to ask.

'Get on with your knitting,' he replied.

When faced with his war memories he shrank into himself. His hazel eyes with the hint of forest-green grew hard and unseeing, like the glass marbles he kept from his childhood. Only last week he put on a balaclava and tried to throttle me with a skipping-rope from behind the kitchen door, but by the time Dr Moss arrived on the scene Otley was reclining in an armchair reading *David Copperfield*.

'I expect it's his nerves; went through it in the war,' said the doctor, writing out a prescription in Ogham.

'But that was a long time ago,' I protested, unable to hide my mean streak. 'We were all in the war one way or another.'

'Oh well,' he said, 'horses for courses. Take the yellow tablets at night and the blue ones in the morning – if these don't work we'll try something else.'

Sky-blue-pink ones, I thought, or green ones with purple spots. That was last week and now Otley wore his blank, moon-face, which meant that the tablets were doing something. His other face was sharp and shrewd and animated by self-interest. But then being a Hawkweed had never been easy: a series of disasters had hit them all at once. Uncle Jack, Myrtle's father, shot himself when Labour won the General Election after the war. Uncle Ben and Aunt Mavis were killed in the blitz and Freda was looked after by Otley's mother Ellen, with grudging help from young sister Janey. Otley's father, Gerald Craven, ran off with a land-girl to grow sugar-beet in East Anglia. It was enough to unhinge a cathedral door and Otley rushed to join the army, lying about his age. He never talked about it.

I took a leaflet out of my pocket and looked at it. 'Three Walks from the centre of Haworth' it proclaimed drunkenly through the creases; so far we had not even managed one, since Otley invariably wanted to be somewhere else.

'It's nearly time for the six o'clock news,' said Otley looking at his wrist-watch. 'If we hurry we might catch it.'

We charged headlong down a farm track offending the sheep with our hooliganism. Soon the disused railway came into view, rusted metal among the yellow ragwort, and we followed it into Low Riding. The little village, thrown up by the Industrial Revolution and then snubbed by the microchip technology, lay stranded like seaweed on the rocks. The Mill House down in the dell – 'Wuthering Depths' to the locals – stood out black as the devil, having escaped a sandblasting in the council's improvement scheme because Aunt Janey said it would weaken the structure.

'Get these pot-holes mended first,' she told them. 'I nearly broke my leg coming back from Bingo last week.'

I tripped and stumbled my way over the half-hidden railway lines as Otley bounded ahead like a kangaroo. He looked round as he reached the garden gate.

'Come on,' he called. 'I don't know why women have to run kay-legged.'

The social worker said that what he needed was an absorbing hobby – well he was interested in espionage but you can't do that at night school. I was his wife, she had said, and it was up to me to put some zip into his life. I leaned gasping on the garden wall. The little blonde elf that Grandad used to call 'Fairyfeet' had somehow turned into a plump, mousy, middle-aged mum. It was a poor outlook for zip! Now if I were a Cleopatra or a Helen of Troy – but mine is not the face to launch a thousand ships. Supermarket trolleys, yes! There was no money to spare for fine clothes and I found myself wondering if Oxfam had any Helen of Troy outfits.

• • • • •

Freda rushed out of the kitchen accompanied by a cloud of steam, damp hair writhing like Medusa locks and blue eyes permanently surprised, like a china doll.

'I expect you're tired going all that way,' she said.

'We didn't make it,' I confessed, standing my boots on an old piece of matting.

'It's farther than you think,' said Freda wafting the steam away with a 'Sunkist Holiday Tours' brochure. Now that she had got Tom Arncliff to the altar Cousin Freda wanted only two things to make her happiness complete – a holiday in Torremolinos and a house with a patio and split-level cooker, like the families on the television commercials who smile at each other while they're eating their cornflakes.

'It looks so nice,' she said, 'with the sun shining on the sugar and milk. Otley always had Bovril on his.'

But Tom had been made redundant when the biscuit factory moved to Clackmannanshire. He could have gone too but declined.

'I'm not going up to Scotland to make bloody biscuits,' he said.

And there was nine-year-old Julian to educate. Julian was born after a reckless adventure in Palermo, when at thirty-five and still unmarried, Freda attended a Fellowship Week of Universal Christians. The cause of her being whispered about and peeped at from behind lace curtains, he was, nevertheless, the apple of her eye. Darkly handsome and, some said out of the corner of their mouths, with the grave demeanour of a mafia Godfather. He also sucked his thumb.

'I hope you're going to take your thumb out of your

mouth long enough to pass your eleven-plus,' his anxious mother said one day. 'Let's have a look at it.'

The thumb came out with a 'plop!' like the popping of a champagne cork as he held it up to the light. It was damp and wrinkled, like a piece of tripe. Freda clucked over it like a broody hen.

'When are you going to stop? That's what I'd like to know.'

Julian thought hard for a minute then made his decision.

'When I'm ten,' he said.

And he could be tiresome. At the age of three in the nursery class they were told to imitate an animal and when, after a lot of elephants and bunny-rabbits, Julian did a stegosaurus nobody knew what it was.

'He has a reading age of fourteen,' his teacher complained when he was seven. 'I don't know what to do with him.'

'He wants to be a nuclear physicist,' Freda told her husband.

'Little sod,' he muttered.

There was a hissing noise and a murky, green soup spluttered on to the stove from a black iron pan. I looked inside.

'It's her witches' brew,' Freda said looking up at the ceiling. 'She'll poison us all one day.'

Cousin Myrtle was our Earth Mother and slept in the attic overlooking Hob Wood so she could see the sap rising in the spring. At fifteen she wanted to run away to the Carolinas with Sergeant Hank Waldorf and was carried screaming off the *Queen Mary* at Liverpool. He had to make do with a lock of hair wrapped up in a recipe for Yorkshire pudding.

'I shall be a nun,' she threatened and devoted herself to being young and beautiful in case he ever came back for her. He didn't.

In a Florence Nightingale mood I decided to take Otley a cup of tea on my way up to change. The stained-glass window on the first landing split up the evening sun making a jigsaw puzzle on the walls. Ira Hawkweed had had it installed in the year of the Great Exhibition; it depicted St George driving a steam engine and Queen Victoria shovelling the coal within a border of smoking mill chimneys. It was said that the dragon tied to the rails was his best friend, Bent Barraclough.

Otley favoured the other attic overlooking the moors in the direction of the early warning station at Skartha. It was just right for his espionage activities and, as he was scouring the horizon with his field-glasses, I touched him on the head so as not to startle him. He jumped and knocked the tea on to the floor.

'Don't patronize me,' he said.

'Dinner's in half an hour,' I said, mopping up the mess with a pair of dirty socks. 'I'm off to have a shower first.'

'Big deal,' he said, spreading out his maps on the table.

'Don't forget to take your tablets,' I reminded him.

'What tablets?' he said.

I withdrew hastily and followed the sound of a tinny gramophone that I knew led to Myrtle's room. Cousin Myrtle supported Greenpeace and it showed. She lived in a riot of swiss-cheese plants reaching upwards and spider plants cascading downwards, grappling each other in the middle. I fought my way through to the bamboo chair where she reclined with a slice of cucumber over each eye. Egg white congealed on her face and neck as the ghost of Al Jolson chased a frantic love song round a wobbling disc. It was a good job he couldn't see her. Suddenly there was a noise like somebody tearing up deck-chair canvases as the needle shot off the record and Myrtle leapt to her feet.

'Did you enjoy the walk?' she wanted to know.

'Yes,' I lied. 'It's lovely when the heather's out.'

'How's the friendly neighbourhood James Bond?' she said, looking at the tea spilled all over my trousers.

'A bit under the weather.'

'There's a good doctor in Bradford, why don't you try him? He's Asian, does a bit of everything.'

'We've tried everything, acupuncture, yoga, homoeopathy, mega-vitamin therapy, herbalism, spiritual healing by post – he doesn't take any notice of them,' I said despairingly.

'Then hit him on the head with the rolling-pin,' she said as she replaced the needle on Al Jolson.

'Freda does the cooking,' I said absent-mindedly. 'And she thinks there's too much sex and violence.'

'On television, yes,' said Myrtle. 'But not here.'

. . . . .

We ate in the kitchen, it being bigger and warmer than the dining-room which was kept for funerals. The holiday brochure lay open at Torremolinos and Tom tried not to look at it as he dealt with his bangers and mash. He was a plain man who liked plain food, but not everybody was pleased with the fare.

'Why don't you use your imagination when you're cooking, Mum?' asked Julian, his rosy-gold face dusted with freckles and innocent as a new-laid egg.

There was a gasp as Freda dropped the dishes into the sink scattering bubbles everywhere.

'I don't get imagination money,' she said.

'Cheeky young devil,' spluttered Tom, chipolatas swirling round in his mouth like washing at the launderette. 'If I'd said that to my mother I'd have got a right leathering.'

'Oriental beef, stuff like that.' Julian went on relentlessly.

'We can't afford English beef never mind anything else,' said Freda biting her lips.

'It's time they did something about the economic situation,' Julian thought. 'The pound fell another half cent against the dollar in New York last night.'

'We don't live in New York, clever dick,' said Tom.

'As long as it buys the same in Keighley market that's all I'm bothered about,' Freda said, wiping up the soap suds.

I had to agree with Julian about home economics at least. Granny Hawkweed had closed the Jubilee Mill down five years ago as she was unable to afford the new machinery to compete with Hong Kong and Taiwan. It was as much a part of the landscape as the millstone grit on Ridings Moor and we ought to find another use for it.

'How about turning the mill into holiday flats?' I asked.

'Good idea!' said Myrtle, swallowing the last of her goat's milk yoghurt. 'I can open a gift shop and sell lavender-bags.'

'And I'll take charge of security,' said Otley all agog.

'Freda can sell home-made cakes,' I went on. 'She's a good cook.'

'When I can get near the stove,' she said, pushing the cauldron aside and sending its contents in green waves over the top.

'Is that frog-spawn?' Julian wanted to know.

'It's my woodland broth,' said Myrtle.

'What's it for?'

'Rejuvenates the system.'

'She means it stirs up the juices,' Tom leered. Now that he spent all his time in the garden he was one with the earth: brown hair, brown eyes and brown bulging muscles. Sitting next to him was like being in the shade of a sturdy young oak.

'That's all you think about,' said Freda with a secret smile.

'I found this old book in the attic,' Myrtle expounded. 'You can do spells and all sorts – anything you want you can get.'

Myrtle was a good advertisement for her way of life. At fifty-five her skin was like a rose petal and her hair, bright as a new penny, fell in a Pre-Raphaelite tumble to her waist when she let it down. She had promised Hank Waldorf never to have it cut.

Tom and Otley went into the front room to watch a documentary about Nicaragua and Julian set to work on a local history project for the school's Open Day.

'You look worried,' Freda said, handing me a cup of tea. 'It's not our fault York Minster got struck by lightning.'

We had gone to the Viking Museum on Otley's fifty-seventh birthday as he fancied that Eric Bloodaxe might be one of his ancestors. Then we looked around the Minster and Otley had put a ten pence piece in the collecting box. We felt a bit ashamed but it was all we had left and that night, 9 July 1984, the south transept went up in flames. We couldn't help thinking that God was trying to tell us something.

'Mike's not in yet,' I explained, but I was getting past caring; like a sponge soaking up water my brain had long since reached saturation point. Just wait until I get my hands on him, the young weasel.

'He's gone up to Jimmy One Eye's to practise his guitar,' Julian informed me without looking up from his books.

'He spends a lot of time with that Dirk Brooklime,' Freda said. 'I don't know what they get up to in that old barn.'

'They're getting up a rock group.'

Everybody knew what Mike was doing except me, but

then I'm only his mother. At the awkward age of fifteen he resented being questioned about his movements. If I asked him where he was going he said 'Out' and if I asked him where he had been he said 'Out'. There were times when I could not be sure whether he was in his room or not and I had to peep through the keyhole to find out. Once he came out and caught me.

'Aren't you ashamed of yourself?' he said.

'Yes,' I lied.

He had been such a sweet little boy, asking me how my back was and telling me to be careful crossing the road, hanging round my neck like a koala bear and snatching cream buns out of my mouth when I was on a diet. Now it seemed that sex or something had reared its ugly head.

THE NEXT day I went down to Keighley to pick up some leaflets about evening classes and, bearing in mind what the social worker had said, I went into Oxfam to see if they had anything with zip in. There was a lot of smelly Crimplene and old tweed skirts, then I found a sweet-pea-coloured chiffon good enough for a Buckingham Palace Garden Party in among the nightgowns by mistake. I had to try it on over my trousers and walking boots but I got the general idea. Then I had my hair lightened at Maison Gillian's and walked back home round by the Wimpey houses.

I took a short cut over the moor by Bilberry Cottage which gave forth its usual odour of rabbit stew and old moleskin trousers. A flounce of red and black told me that the gypsies were in and I called out to them over the mountain of dead television sets outside their front door.

'Anybody home?'

There was a scuffling noise and one of last year's conkers hit me on the head. That Tansy, saucy little madam, it was time she went to school. I turned away fuming, then I remembered the time I set fire to the muckstack at Doncaster with a piece of burning tarband, and Granny tried to put it out with a leaking bucket. I decided not to wallop her after all.

I came out into Meadow Lane by the Primitive Methodist Chapel; it had been built next door to The Flying Shuttle so that the old Ranters could lie in wait for the godless as they staggered out of the pub on a Sunday afternoon. Granny Blinks at the corner shop was just locking up and across the derelict railway station I could see Stalin busy with his pigs which he kept in the Ladies' waiting room. The old packhorse trail, an ancient right of way, bisected our kitchen garden and straddled the beck on a humpbacked bridge. In wet weather the walkers filed past with their waterproofs over their backpacks like a stream of multi-coloured humpbacked goblins. It was deserted now but for Kit Constable, the local Michelangelo, doing yet another version of Ousel Beck.

.....

Although I say it myself I did look nice that evening. Tom leered and Julian took his thumb out of his mouth so that I felt I had to apologize.

'You have to dress up now and again for a change.'

'That's true,' Tom said, looking in Freda's direction.

'It's nice,' said Freda, ignoring him.

Otley had his other face on and was in a mean mood.

'What difference does it make?' he wanted to know. 'We all end up the same way – six feet under. How much was it?'

I told him twenty-five pounds and asked him to pay for it – it's the only way I can make any money these days.

'What did you do today?' I asked conversationally.

'Bird-watching,' he said. 'Why, have you missed me?'

'Yes,' I lied.

Myrtle came back from a CND meeting, hair sparkling like a copper pan-scrubber. Dumping a white glutinous mass on to a plate of salad she began to eat.

'What's that?' said Julian.

'It's quark.'

'Ugh!'

'It's only cheese,' Myrtle said with a bean-sprout sticking out of the corner of her mouth. Julian fixed her with a stare.

'Then why don't they call it cheese?'

'Don't be rude,' said Freda.

'Miss Allen said if we wanted to know anything we had to ask.'

There seemed to be no answer to that so Myrtle told us about their plans for a demo on Battle of Britain day. Greenpeace and Friends of the Earth were to meet CND at Rombald's statue in the town square, and they were marching to the early warning station at Skartha thirty miles away.

'What for?' said Freda.

'Because,' Myrtle went on, 'they are entertaining the United States Air Force, and as we are in favour of unilateral disarmament we want to make our views known to the authorities.'

'Oh,' said Freda.

'They don't care,' said Otley. 'Silly sods are wasting their time!'

'Watch your language in front of children!' Freda said, squirting washing-up liquid all over the window as she turned round.

'I've a good mind to write to the Admiralty,' Julian said out of the blue. 'We've hardly any ships left now.'

'He's not a child, he's a seventy-year-old midget,' Tom said.

'Well if I join the navy what do they expect me to do with an old bath-tub like we've got?'

'Not much,' agreed Otley.

'Russia and America are building up an invincible nuclear armada,' said Julian aggrieved. 'I shall join them.'

'Oh shut up Einstein,' said Tom.

Just then the door slammed and as nobody came in we knew it must be Mike. I smiled, trying to be like the ideal mother in the women's magazines but it wasn't easy.

We washed up the dishes and then switched on the box for our daily dose of catastrophe – dock strike, underground train crash, salmonella poisoning, plane crash, TUC to rejoin Neddy.

'The base lending rate is down to eleven per cent,' Julian pointed out.

'Shut up!' said Tom.

I escaped as soon as I could to the privacy of my room and the comfort of my old dressing-gown. Luckily there were enough rooms in the old house for everybody to have one, which was just as well as the Hawkweeds were not the sort of family to go for this togetherness stuff. Later on I knocked on Mike's door.

'Everything all right?' I asked nonchalantly.

'Of course it is,' he said through the closed door.

'Where have you been?'

'Out.'

'With Dirk Brooklime?' I asked fearfully.

'Yes.'

The door remained closed so I had to look through the key-hole.

'What doing?' I asked in a strangled voice due to my position.

'Stop peeping through the keyhole,' he said.

'Good night then,' I said. 'See you tomorrow.'

'Good night.'

Otley was studying the moon through his binoculars and as the door was open I tried to tiptoe past without being seen.

'Just come and look at this,' he called out, handing me the glasses. I raised them to my eyes and saw nothing but a white blur.

'I can see better without them,' I said, handing them back.

'No you can't,' he said.

'Yes I can.'

'Must be something wrong with your eyes then.'

'Good night.'

'Good night.'

Myrtle was listening to 'Carolina Moon' when I went in to give her the garden party creation. I parted with it reluctantly but it was more her than me. She thanked me and said what a good idea it was to convert the mill into holiday flats. The house was a ready-made museum being still the same as Granny Hawkweed had left it when she died of shock from having to close the mill down. All that mahogany and stained glass would be worth a fortune if we ever wanted to sell it. Then there was that dusty old shoe box full of saucy postcards from Blackpool and Bridlington; people were collecting them now. It was all in the best of Victorian bad taste. We might even get on the *Antiques Roadshow*. And what price would they put on broken hearts and shattered dreams? 'Skreek-skrawk' went the scratchy old record and I made for the door before the needle shot off and set my teeth on edge. In my haste I got entangled in the cascading spider plants and brought one crashing down on my head.

'They breed like rabbits,' she said apologetically.

In the safety of my own room I poured out a hot drink from a flask and sat by the open window before turning in for the night. The Man in the Moon looked down at me and I thought he seemed to be laughing.

. . . . .

The next morning I waylaid Mike in the hall to assure myself that I really did have a son and then showed Otley the leaflet about evening classes.

'There's no need for anybody to be bored,' I told him. There was something for everybody, from plumbing to icing wedding cakes, and although I am not mechanically minded myself, in a fit of generosity I offered to accompany him to car maintenance classes.

'What's the matter,' he said. 'Are you so hard up for a friend that you want me?'

Then we went through the 'Come and join us' programme and the choice was dazzling. As well as Weight Watching and Tatting there was Ukrainian Dancing, Barbershop Singing, Scrabble, Transcendental Meditating and a Fungus Weekend with Friends of the Earth.

'I'll do shark fishing,' Otley decided.

'What, here in Keighley?' I said.

'I expect they go down to Cornwall,' he replied, giving me a withering look.

'That'll be nice,' I said amiably. 'Have you got a good strong fishing-rod? That one you had in the Boy Scouts won't do.'

'Of course I haven't,' he said as if I were stark raving mad.

He said he would hire some equipment from the club until he was sure it was what he wanted and I agreed that it was the sensible thing to do. I made some more tea and scrambled three eggs and said would he mind having a word with Mike that evening about his odd behaviour.

'What odd behaviour?' he wanted to know. Then he apologized for being such a pig; he couldn't help it, something got into him. I patted him on the forehead and said it didn't matter.

'All right Mary Poppins,' he said.

Across the road in Bobbin Yard, Kit Constable was setting up his easel. Stockily-built and with square, capable hands he was more like a prize-fighter than an artist. If I were younger, I thought, and in possession of a heart, it would be missing a beat right now. The signals he sent out spelt 'Danger' to the unwary female but he would be an asset when it came to putting Low Riding on the tourist map. I watched him as he rapidly sketched a group of children on their way to school and then tore it up and threw it away.

.....

I met Granny Blinks on my way to post a letter and she asked me how Otley was.

'He's fine,' I lied. 'And Mike's doing so well at school he doesn't want to leave.'

'That's funny,' she said. 'Dirk Brooklime said he was leaving at Christmas and they're going on the stage.'

'He must have made a mistake,' I said. 'Must be somebody else.' I tried not to show my concern but instead of going straight home I went round by Jimmy One Eye's to see if I could see Dirk. Old Jimmy, who looked like a frog, lashed out at his herd of cows with a length of blackthorn and focused his one eye on me as I approached.

'Good morning Mr . . . er . . . Brooklime,' I stopped myself from saying Mr One Eye just in time. 'Is Dirk in?'

'What's he bin up to, he's nobbut a bairn,' he said.

'Nothing,' I assured him. 'He's a friend of Mike, my son.'

'Oh, aye!' he said, flicking a lump of cow muck out of his ear. 'He'll be inside having a sit down.'

I picked my way across the uneven cobbles, dodging an assortment of disembodied wheels and rusting machines. Mrs Brooklime saw me from the mullioned window and opened the door to let me in. Fat and rosy, she resembled her husband in every way and I found it easy to imagine them coupling on a water-lily leaf.

The stone-flagged kitchen floor was strewn with hooky rugs which she and her sister made on the long, dark winter nights. Dirk sprawled in a comfortable chair, his legs straddling a fearsome hound black as the ace of spades. It was obvious he took after his mother, Mrs Brooklime's sister. The Brooklimes had given up all hope of having a family until Floradora moved in with them – then they hit upon a sensible solution. Old customs die hard and in days of yore if there was no legitimate heir to succeed to your cabbage patch you got one in any way you could.

'I'm Mike's mother,' I said. 'I was just passing by.'

He smirked at this because the farm was half a mile from the road and there was no way you could just pass by.

'Oh! Yeah!' he said like Clint Eastwood, his eyes narrowed.

'He comes up here a lot doesn't he?'

'They enjoy themselves getting up their stage act,' said Mrs Brooklime, putting a lardy cake into the oven.

'What stage act?'

Dirk unwound himself to his full height, six feet of blond beefcake towering over me.

'We've rigged a disco up in the old barn – you can't complain of the noise out here,' he said accusingly.

'Mike told me all about it,' I lied, feeling ashamed of myself for having run out screaming into the night when the racket had brought on a migraine.

'They write their own songs,' said Mrs Brooklime.

'What about?' I felt obliged to ask.

'Inner-city decay, the fascist oppression of our jackbooted overlords.'

'Sounds great,' I said, picking up my handbag to go.

'And the ingrained sexist attitude of the petty bourgeoisie.'

'I don't know what he's on about half the time but it's better than mugging old ladies,' Mrs Brooklime philosophized.

'We can do Friday nights at the Shuttle,' Dirk went on. 'Just for expenses.'

The drug problem suddenly seemed relevant to Low Riding and I felt I ought to offer some advice.

'Well, don't let anybody slip anything into your drinks,' I said, thinking this would cover all eventualities. I left with his reckless laughter ringing in my ears.

I PICKED UP Otley's tablets from the chemist and then called at Station Road to see Aunt Janey. She lived at number two and her friend Stalin lived at number four; the house in between remained empty as she liked him to keep his distance. Stalin once raised broiler chickens but people wrote to the council complaining of the smell so he got rid of them and got some pigs instead.

Stalin was the spitting image of 'Uncle Joe' with his road-sweeper moustache and old briar pipe and he wore the same enigmatic smile, as if he knew something the rest of us didn't. The truth was he had a tidy sum tucked away for a rainy day, donated by the good folk of Low Riding who had kept his pigs for years; they looked down their noses at him when he knocked on the door with his smelly bucket and old corduroys tied up with string, but good-naturedly filled his bucket up for him all the same.

'If I were as handsome as him,' said Aunt Janey, 'I'd never be mucky.'

Dressed in a neat blue overall, eyes bright as shoe-buttons, she made quick, fluttering movements like an excited budgie. Patting cushions here, straightening pictures there, crocheting lace doilies and squirting lemon-scented aerosols everywhere. She preferred her little terraced house as it was easy to keep warm in winter, and had been glad to get away from the mill house, with its stuffed birds and aspidistras, as soon as she could after the funeral.

'Pooh!' said Stalin as he called to pick up his sandwiches. 'Have you been squirting that stuff over them again?'

Aunt Janey handed him the sandwiches tied up in a red spotted handkerchief on the end of a stick.

'Get away with you,' she said. 'It's better than pigs any day.'

Yes, she would give us a hand with the flats but she couldn't see why anybody would want to stay here with Haworth just up the road. I told her that the Village Heritage Trust would help with a grant if we could come up with some village heritage.

'How's Otley?' she said, sniffing.

'Up and down,' I told her.

'Why don't you go away for a nice holiday?' she said, straightening the curtains. 'Don't you get fed up of him sitting in the attic spying on everybody?'

'Yes.'

'It's nice at Scarborough near the pier.'

I said he wouldn't go to the seaside because of the sewage on the beach. Shark fishing he might try if they took him far enough out.

'Lake District's nice,' she said.

I reminded her of the fall-out from Sellafield and the sheep eating all Wordsworth's daffodils.

'Bournemouth's nice down by the Chines,' she said.

Had she forgotten it was too far by coach and he wouldn't pay the exorbitant train fares? Besides, the last time he went, there were too many squirrels in Fisherman's Walk and they ran off with his salted peanuts.

'You don't try,' she said accusingly. 'Poor soul needs a good holiday.'

. . . . .

Julian came home from school with some exciting news for us. Ours was the first cotton mill in Yorkshire; they brought bales from the Carolinas up the Leeds and Liverpool Canal, then in the American Civil War when they couldn't get cotton they went over to wool. At the mention of Carolina, Myrtle burnt her nut rissoles to a frazzle in the wok and wondered aloud if there might be something in the lumber room about it.

'And,' said Julian, 'Karl Marx slept at the pub one night, when he was going to Manchester to see Fred.'

'Listen at Mastermind!' said Tom through his toad-in-the-hole.

'It used to be The King's Head – but he got them to change it to The Flying Shuttle,' Julian went on.

Later on Myrtle and I went up to the lumber room while the others were watching *The Twilight Zone* on the television and among the dusty old books and portraits of defunct Hawkweeds we found a Bill of Lading for the delivery of raw cotton from Georgetown, South Carolina and a cutting from the *Ridings Mercury* about a Mr Karl Marx, a foreign gentleman engaged in the study of 'manufactories', who had expressed a desire to see the mill.

We could have two plaques put up, it was decided later, then inform the Russian and American Embassies of our enterprise. We could do guided walks to Top Withens I suggested eagerly.

'Will the Russians be able to walk all that way with those big overcoats on?' Julian wanted to know.

Mike started talking to us, saying it had given him a good idea for a song, and Otley sensed it was a good opportunity for him to practise some international espionage. Myrtle melted down a lump of beeswax and wrote 'Hank Waldorf' on it with a pin on one side and her lucky numbers on the other side, then stuck it on to a map of South Carolina and put it under her pillow to see what she dreamed about. She dreamed about Tom Selleck in *Magnum*.

THE FOLLOWING Saturday Freda and I went to Keighley to see the CND march off. Myrtle wore her Italian army trousers, camouflage jacket, woolly hat and yellow Derriboots and carried a bright red rucksack filled with Marmite sandwiches, muesli bars, goat's milk yoghurt, dates and apples and a toilet roll.

A crowd gathered round Giant Rombald's statue in the shopping precinct and somebody had painted the CND sign on his behind.

'I always thought that was Geoff Capes,' said Freda.

It started to drizzle and after a bearded marshal like Jesus in a jogging suit had harangued them through a megaphone, the demonstrators moved off in a bedraggled line like the Vietnamese Boat People.

'Better her than me,' observed Freda as we went round Boots looking for the corn plasters.

After a coffee and a sit-down in the Co-op we got the Sunday joint and then went to see what they had at Oxfam. I found a respectable copy of Froissart's *Chronicles* for twenty-five pence and a dog-eared score of *The Student Prince* that reminded me of a holiday in Heidelberg when Otley and I were human beings, a peasant blouse and a yellow nylon wig which would be all right when it was washed. What fun it would be to go skipping over the hills like *The Sound of Music*. I wondered if they had any lederhosen to fit Otley.

'I don't know how you can wear them,' said Freda.

'How d'you mean?' I said, knowing very well.

'Dead men's shoes,' she said, looking down her nose.

I took no notice. I remembered Gran saying they had to wait until somebody died before they could have a bed or a knife and fork. I got a pile of old *Beanos* and some *National Geographic* magazines for Julian then we took the bus home, winding slowly along the leafy lanes, bright with rose-hips and elderberries and the beck, we noticed, choking to death on old mattresses and rusty bedsteads.

. . . . .

When we got home the men were watching *Grandstand* and waiting for their tea.

'What would you do,' Freda said, 'if I were struck by lightning?'

'I expect Aunt Janey would make it,' said Julian.

I stayed in that evening while the others went to the Shuttle and after tucking Julian in with an elderly *Private Eye* I went to look through the keyhole to see if Mike was in.

'He's gone up to Jimmy One Eye's,' Julian shouted as if he knew what I was doing. 'They're having a disco.'

Otley seemed very pleased with himself when they came

in and Freda said I had better watch out because Nancy Blinks, the barmaid, was after him.

'Couldn't keep her hands off him!'

I refrained from saying she could have him and went to make some cocoa and sandwiches. We talked until midnight then the door slammed and nobody came in so we knew Mike was back and it was all right to go to bed.

As I stood at the open window a jet screamed over on its way to Skartha and I wondered if Myrtle was enjoying her demonstration. Then there was the sound of laughter and a car door opened and shut as Kit Constable took leave of his friends. He really was something and I had read that a little flirtation could liven up a stale marriage. If my husband took a fancy to Nancy it might give Mike a cue for a song too. I looked at the yellow wig drying on the bedpost and wondered if Kit liked fräuleins.

The next day was the harvest festival so Freda, Aunt Janey and I went to the afternoon service but here I have to admit that when I was a child religion gave me a splitting headache. They didn't call them Ranters for nothing and I was always the first to volunteer to go round the back and pump the organ. Then those Sunday evening processions! Mother and Father, Grandmother and Grandfather and Great Aunt Martha done up like a dog's dinner, and the church bells ding-donging in your ears all the way – they enjoyed it but as far as I was concerned God had dropped a clanger.

Mike graced us with his presence at meal times and seemed quite friendly. How was dad these days? Would we like him and Dirk to do 'An Evening with Karl Marx' when we got the plaque up at the Shuttle? Could we lend him some money and would I mend his jeans as he'd torn them on the barbed-wire coming through Fitchet fields? He then retired to his room and locked the door.

Later, in the hour of limbo, I decided to try on my fräulein outfit.

'Anyone for a skip through the heather?' I inquired gaily.

'Good God! you look like Danny La Rue,' said Otley.

Tom leered and Freda drew his attention to the holiday brochure and asked him what size espadrilles he would require. Julian said nothing, he was watching *The Money Programme*.

'Miss Armitage says I have to put some zip into your life.'

'Miss Armitage is a prat.'

'She wants us to go and see her this week.'

'Tell her to get stuffed.'

'She's only trying to help.'

'Tell her to look after that snotty-nosed kid of hers; he could do with a good square meal by the look of him,' Otley went on.

'He can't help it if he's got adenoids and his mum neglects him,' Julian said, taking his thumb out of his mouth for a minute.

'Shut up!' said Tom.

I went – not so much skipping through the heather as crawling; clutching at the clumps of bracken I hauled myself up to the Druids' circle and collapsed, too tired to eat my sesame crunch. I took out my book of poems by Currer, Ellis and Acton Bell and opened it at a little-known one by the latter.

> Because the road is rough and long,
> Shall we despise the skylark's song?

That's true, I remember thinking before I fell asleep.

. . . . .

The sun was setting when I awoke and I stumbled my way

down the moor to the beck. Kit Constable had set up his easel beside a waterfall and was trying to capture the blaze of colour reflected in the sparkling water.

'Gorgeous sunset,' I remarked, hoping that he would recognize in me a kindred spirit. He added a few blobs of orange and violet to the canvas and stood back to admire the effect.

'I don't know why I bother, nobody buys them,' he complained.

'Have you tried putting people in, instead of just grass and trees?' I asked him.

'I can't draw people,' he said shamefaced.

'Neither could Lowry,' I pointed out.

'Who do you suggest I use for a model?' he said, looking me up and down. I told him I didn't mean that arty-crafty stuff with nudes.

'Some local colour,' I said. 'Stalin with his pigs, old Granny Blinks – that sort of thing.'

'Oh!' His dark eyes lost their sparkle for a moment and then it came back as he told me my wig was coming off; he had a good selection at home if I would like to try them on, he said.

We followed the beck into the village and I found him easy to talk to but his nearness disturbed me. I imagined that artists were airy, ethereal creatures and here I was enveloped in an earthy, animal magnetism that was entirely unexpected.

'Allow me,' he said, holding out his arm at an awkward stile, but I nipped smartly over. Although I was enjoying the attention and hoped to have more of it, the sort of thing I had in my mind was more in the nature of a Dante and Beatrice affair, or Heloise and Abelard after he had been unmanned. I loved writing letters and would like someone to send me love poems from a thousand miles away.

'I've seen you at the window,' he said, touching my hand.
I started as if from an electric shock.
'I've seen you,' I said, letting my hand stay touched.

'I'M FED up with this miserable dump,' said Otley the next morning with his other face on.

'Have you had your tablets?' I asked him.

'Sod the tablets,' he said.

'I thought you were going shark fishing,' I said, handing him a cup of tea and being careful to approach him from the front as you would a fractious horse.

'What's the point of going on holiday, you've only got to come back again,' he said, kicking a patchwork tortoise that Mike gave me for Christmas.

'Do you the world of good – wrestling with nature,' I said. 'I'll come as well if you like.'

'I want to get away from you,' he said.

'Oh! all right.'

I breathed a sigh of relief. Every year I watched the holiday-makers struggling back with their luggage, bankrupt and exhausted, and thought how pleasant it was to sit in the shade of a fragrant lime tree with a cool drink and a book. It was such an occasion when Kit first called on us.

> 'A Flask of Wine, a Book of Verse – and Thou
> Beside me singing in the Wilderness –'

He recited, his arms spread out and his hands gripping the garden gate like a preacher in the pulpit. I was a bit embarrassed and looked up at the sky, saying I thought it looked like rain. Freda called him in for some tea and fell under his spell.

'He's like that with all the women,' Tom warned her. 'Somebody saw Nancy Blinks coming out of Bobbin Yard with her hair all over the place.'

'I know,' said Freda.

Kit said he had a friend, a sculptor in Bradford, who could do us a Karl Marx cheap as he had some old iron left over from the arrangement he did for the Arts Council. Those among us who were of the communist persuasion were very pleased but the fascist tendency led by Billy Delph, the local gauleiter, demanded a statue of Mussolini because there had been an Italian Prisoner of War Camp in Fitchet fields – the barbed-wire was there to prove it. Kit thought he might be able to get hold of some bricks when the council knocked one of the mill chimneys down.

'Knock it down yourself,' they told him.

'Give us a chance,' he pleaded. 'I'm only human.'

• • • • •

When Kit had finished the portrait of Stalin he asked me over to look at it. He had turned the weaver's cottage into a studio flat and showroom, full of pine and cane furniture; it was light and airy, a pleasant change from our solid mahogany. He carefully unveiled the painting and yes, he was right, he couldn't draw people. Posed outside the Ladies' waiting room on the derelict platform, Stalin had one leg longer than the other and a right arm seemingly broken in three places. Eileen, his favourite pig, standing to attention by his side was a bright, shining pink like a piggy-bank, pot-legged and glass-eyed.

'What do you think of it?' he asked.

'It's lovely,' I lied.

He covered it up again and we ate cheese and pickles and drank red plonk leaning over the table like Toulouse-Lautrec at the Moulin Rouge. Then he put on a record of *Carmina Burana* and by the time it got to the bit where the nuns and monks are having a medieval orgy, I found my eyelashes were getting entangled with the hairs on his chest. I thought it was time to go.

'Where have you been to?' Otley wanted to know.

'Out,' I said, wondering if he was jealous.

'I can't find a clean shirt anywhere,' he said.

Just then Myrtle came back from the demo with blistered feet and mud-caked trousers. They had sat down in the road at Skartha singing 'We shall not be moved' until the police sent in a snatch-squad and took them to the local nick for the night. When they were let out the next day they cleaned themselves up in a Public Convenience and went to Harrogate for a few days.

'The little people have to make their voices heard,' she said, sorting out some leaflets. I had to agree but I'm too lazy to do anything about it. Otley said it would make no difference as both the Russians and Americans would vaporize us if it suited them, missile site or not.

'And if the Japs sent you on a long march like that you wouldn't want to go!' said Julian.

We watched a programme on the box about food and health. 'You are what you eat', it told us, and we were all too fat.

'That's true,' said Myrtle.

Why was it, inquired the front man, that in face of all the evidence it was taking us so long to change our diet to a healthy one.

'Because we're ignorant bastards,' said Otley. 'Scum of the earth like the Duke of Wellington said.'

'Language!' said Freda.

'Well look at May,' he said, nodding in my direction.

'What about May?'

'Overweight and undersexed, like a giant panda,' he said.

All eyes turned on me and feeling like a discarded cuddly toy, I said good night and crept up to my den.

. . . . .

The next day Otley and I went to Miss Armitage for a finger-wagging session, sneaking in and out again in case anybody saw us, like a couple of senile delinquents. I mustn't mind if he strayed, she said, he was at a funny age. I said I didn't mind and she looked disappointed; I explained that I was at a funny age as well.

'I'm not going there again for you to show me up,' said Otley.

We paid the rates at the Town Hall and then called at the library for a book on shark fishing. There wasn't one so he got *The Life and Times of Genghis Khan* instead. On the way out I stopped to look at a poster about a course on women's history: suffragettes, Victorian millgirls and ladies bountiful. Otley seemed embarrassed.

'What's the matter?' he said. 'Do you want to be a person?'

We had pizza and chips before calling in to see the doctor for some more tablets. He picked up a huge book and went half-way through it before finding what he wanted.

'I'm only giving you thirty of these,' he said. 'They're forty pounds for a hundred.'

Instead of strangling him we thanked him and got up to go.

'And how's Mr Craven these days?' he inquired.

'I'm all right,' said Otley. 'It's my bloody wife.'

We caught the bus home as Otley had given up driving for the time being, which was a relief as he had a tendency to tear up and down the motorways at ninety miles an hour, grumbling all the time, while I lay on the back seat with a migraine. It was a nice change lurching about at the front of the top deck, like a mahout on an elephant. Otley apologized for being such a pig. He didn't mean it, his tongue ran away with him that's all. That was true, he was a decent enough chap for a madman. I squeezed his hand and offered him a Polo mint.

'You know that blue striped shirt with the detachable collar?'

'Yes,' I assured him.

'Well where is it?'

After such an eventful day it was good to relax in front of the box. There was a wildlife documentary about copulating rhinos, then talking heads making chopping movements with their thumbs up, Burt Lancaster in *Elmer Gantry*, and a piece about the tombs of the Pharaohs in which an elderly gentleman with glass eyes and a face like the Dead Sea Scrolls gave us the benefit of his wisdom.

'Who's that?' asked Julian. 'He talks like a fossil.'

I had seen Joan Crawford in *Mildred Pierce* five times so I excused myself and went to my room to read. Kit was on my mind and I went to the window to see what he was doing. He was doing nothing so I said good night to the Man in the Moon and went to bed before I turned into a werewolf.

THAT WEEK there was a fancy-dress dance in aid of the Royal National Life-boat Institution.

'I never knew we had a lifeboat in Keighley,' said Aunt Janey.

I went as Dick Whittington, borrowing Stalin's red and white spotted kerchief, and Otley went as the Laughing Cavalier. He had been shut up in his room all week but we didn't worry too much; he did that once before and never went out for six months, then packed his bags and went on holiday to Majorca.

Nancy went as Nell Gwynne and sat in a corner eating potted meat sandwiches with the Laughing Cavalier for most of the time. By the end of the hokey cokey we had to sit down and get the sausage-rolls off our feet, so Percy Dredger from the Water Board did an impression of Gene Kelly doing 'Singin' in the Rain'.

'It's a grand day for t'watter,' he said, looking up at the rain battering the windows.

Freda as a harem dancer and Tom as the Sultan of Zanzibar looked a bit out of place standing at the bus stop soaking wet.

'I'm going home,' she said. 'Everybody's looking at us.'

Myrtle agreed. She was the Quality Street lady and her crinoline made out of toffee papers came unstuck and went floating down the gutter blocking up the drains. When I got in they were playing Scrabble with one eye and watching *Bride of Frankenstein* with the other.

'Don't ask us to get dressed up again,' said Tom. 'Making a laughing-stock of ourselves.'

'I didn't ask you,' I had to point out.

They made ninety-nine pounds for the brave men of the sea – enough to buy sixty-six pairs of seaboot socks.

Otley came home with the milk the morning after the dance, and well-wishers told me that there were ostrich feathers in the Michaelmas daisies behind Granny Blinks's shop. I was urged to go and see for myself.

'You'll come to a bad end just like your mother!' said Granny Blinks to her wayward grandchild. Nancy's mother was divorced and living in Harrogate. A place where devils were spawned in the sulphur springs thought the old lady.

'I fainted and Mr Craven brought me home,' said Nancy who was knitting a bikini, candy-floss hair falling into her eyes and lips gleaming like a newly painted pillarbox.

Why hadn't she knocked on the door we wanted to know. It seemed that Mr Craven was clearing the garden of litter when a dog ran off with his hat so they went to look for it.

'Oh!' I said.

'And what's that you're knitting?' asked Granny Blinks who was against knitting and fornicating on a Sunday.

'It's a new dishcloth,' said Nancy. 'Your old one's worn out.'

'She'll come to a bad end,' said Granny. 'Would you like a cup of tea?'

. . . . .

Otley was a lot more cheerful after that and talked about going back to work. Something adventurous, not the Civil Service again – he'd had enough of those creeps – something like diving for sunken treasure in the Spanish Main, but when he found he was too old to go on a training course he got a metal-detector and went up on the moors. He came back with some metal rings off ginger-beer cans and an old threepenny-bit which he threw at my patchwork tortoise.

'You might as well be dead as live here,' he complained. 'No buried treasure, nothing.'

It was good, healthy exercise in the fresh air, we told him, and he couldn't expect to find it at the first attempt. We'd go with him next time and take some sandwiches. He didn't like the sound of that.

'River crossings are best,' said Julian. 'Where their swords fell in the water after a skirmish.'

'Shut up, clever dick,' said Tom.

'Well I can't help it if I'm brainy,' Julian protested.

'And I can't help it if I'm a bully,' said Tom.

I thought it was time to go and dead-head the roses and see if there were any ramblers looking for the right of way into Hob Wood. There were none but I found Kit sketching Tansy under a sycamore tree, her arms and legs skittling in all directions like a young foal. He made a few lightning strokes then handed her a toffee-apple.

'I like it,' she said. 'It's better than ferreting.'

'I've sold *Stalin*,' Kit told me. 'I owe you a drink.'

'No you don't,' I said, thinking of that awful plonk. 'But thanks.'

We talked for a while until it started to rain. The gypsies collected Tansy and Kit said he would have to go and take his paintings in. Yes, I said, we would all go over for a drink later on. For some reason he blew down the back of my neck and against my better judgement I liked it.

Myrtle wore the floaty chiffon and let her hair down and Kit saw her as the Lady of the Lake. Would she mind standing in Ousel Beck so that he could paint her? Not at all, said Myrtle, it was as she had always seen herself. How clever of him to read her mind!

'You'll get your death of cold,' said Freda.

'I'll put my green wellies on and my Damart underwear,' said Myrtle. 'And I'll take a flask of soup and a hot-water bottle.'

'Tread softly, you tread on my dreams,' Kit said, pouring out wine from an unlabelled bottle.

'It tastes like red biddy,' whispered Tom.

'Shh . . .!' said Freda, pouring hers into an umbrella palm.

We admired the painting of Tansy with one leg sticking out at right angles and eyes looking in different directions like a Picasso.

'Is that her ear or is it fungus on the tree?' asked Freda.

'It's her nose,' said Kit.

'Oh!' Freda said, nodding in sympathy.

'If this one sells I'm sticking to people,' Kit decided.

Otley was on his best behaviour with his public face on, rational and responsible, and when I was sick from the lethal combination of gooey white Brie, soggy white baps and vinegary plonk, he put his arm round me as if I were a retarded chimpanzee.

'I'll look after her,' he said. 'It's her age, poor soul.'

Kit told us that Karl Marx and Mussolini had been installed and that the children thought they were adventure playgrounds and the dogs barked at them; furthermore somebody had written 'Mrs Brown' on Queen Victoria's statue on the village green and it wouldn't come off. We would have to complain to the council.

Before leaving Bobbin Yard we had a look at the mill as they planned to begin the conversion. There was a lot of rubble lying about and Freda ricked her ankle. Myrtle caught her flounces in the cement-mixer and I was sick again. We arrived home in a sorry state. Julian was watching *Panorama* and turned to Mike in disgust:

'They're not fit to be let out,' he said.

'I know,' said Mike. 'There's all these people starving in Africa and they can't even walk across the road.'

'Bedtime,' shouted Tom but nobody took any notice.

. . . . .

Christmas came and went and we all put on funny hats and pretended we loved each other. Julian read *Jane Eyre* in his. In January a heavy fall of snow wrapped us in a hush, and in the sensory deprivation that followed it was easy to think that you were dead. While we hid away in our favourite corners trying to keep warm, Otley took to walking on the moors.

'You're mad going out in this,' I told him.

'I'm mad if I don't go out in it,' he said.

'Supposing you don't come back?'

'Save you five hundred pounds for the funeral.'

He affected a demeanour like that of Captain Oates walking off into the blizzard and we were impressed until Mike told us he had seen him tobogganing down Ridings Fell with Nancy Blinks. After that we stopped worrying.

'Why don't you do something?' Myrtle said, stirring her broth like one of the witches from *Macbeth*. 'Everybody's talking about him and Nancy Blinks.'

'Let them talk,' I said. 'I've got past caring.'

'You don't mean that.'

'I do mean that – she might do him more good than a psychiatrist.'

The buses stopped running and we slithered our way around in shapeless bundles, like figures in a Breughel landscape. Then we lay at night cocooned like chrysalids waiting to emerge as butterflies in the spring. This butterfly at least would need a helping hand and we thought a week at a health farm might work. The men were dumbfounded. Who was going to get their dinner they wanted to know.

'Nancy can get yours,' I told Otley.

'Nancy?'

He clearly only connected her with frolicking in the snow. The others, we thought, could go to Aunt Janey's.

'She's got no imagination, she's worse than Mum,' said Julian.

'And what if Stalin comes with his smelly bucket?' said Mike.

It seemed that we would have to have a health week at home and I said I would look in the library for a do-it-yourself book.

'Will you take *Genghis Khan* back and bring *Mein Kampf* if they've got it?' said Otley.

'What do you want that for?' I asked.

'Well I fought the bloody war now I want to find out what it was all about,' he said.

Presently the snows melted and sixty-five miles an hour blasts roared down from the moors. Whinooks, Otley called them – like the chinooks in the Rockies but blowing down off the whin. It was enough to drive a man mad, he said, and would I hurry up and get *Mein Kampf*. It must be nice to have your own personal lackey, I thought, but I had to get my weight down anyway. I couldn't find *Mein Kampf* on the shelves, but I picked up a book by Hitler's doctor and then put it back again quick; it seemed to be a record of his bowel movements.

When I asked at the desk for *Mein Kampf* everything went quiet and they said I had to see the Librarian in a little room. He peered at me over his bifocals and asked for my name and address.

'How long have you lived here?' he wanted to know.

'All my life,' I said.

'Where were your mother and father born?' he asked.

'Quarry Bottoms,' I said.

'Have you any political affiliations?' he asked.

'No.'

'Then why do you want this book?'

'It's not for me, it's for my husband,' I said, getting annoyed.

'And what does he do?'

'Nothing – he's mad.'

He jumped back as if he had discovered a cobra curled up in his favourite slippers, then asked me to fill in a form. He wrote something in a little black book and then locked it away in a drawer and handed me *Mein Kampf* in brown wrapping paper.

'And don't forget to bring it back,' he warned.

I had to push my way through a group of people gathered at the desk on the way out. There was a lot of muttering and mumbling.

'Fascist pig!' somebody said.

Somebody else stamped my forehead with the date-stamp.

'Look here!' I said defending myself, 'I read *Farmer's Weekly* as well but I haven't got swine-fever.'

'How do we know?' they said.

I did my shopping looking over my shoulder to see if I was being followed and took the bus back instead of walking. I handed Otley the book and he looked askance at it. What a paltry thing it was, he thought it would be bigger than that, all the trouble it caused.

'And I nearly got lynched,' I told him. 'Go and get your own books in future.'

'You're a selfish little madam,' he said.

OUR GRANT came through from the Village Heritage Trust and the council had given permission for the mill to be converted into flats for holiday lettings. Freda was prepared to live in as caretaker if Tom would only take her to Torremolinos first, before the season started.

'You'll have to do the cooking then,' Tom said anxiously. 'You know I don't like that greasy dago muck.' He was partial to treacle pudding and could become irritable if deprived of it for any length of time. Freda swore that if he asked her to make some in Torremolinos she would put instant Locktite glue in it instead of golden syrup.

It was agreed that we would stay in the old house with Myrtle, living on the top floor and showing the main rooms to the public as a typical nineteenth-century mill owner's establishment.

A village moot was held under the Shire Oak in Fitchet

fields, a meeting place from the time the first Anglo-Saxons found their way into our hidden valleys. Things could not be much worse than they were now and our plans were generally approved. A fancy-dress ball would be nice, we thought, to celebrate our success. Jimmy One Eye objected, saying he wasn't playing silly buggers for anybody, then the company dispersed.

I had noticed the gypsies were not there and as it was a fine, warm evening I took a walk up to Bilberry Cottage. Zelda answered my knock and I invited myself in. I had often wondered what it was like inside. There was a cauldron of rabbit stew bubbling away on the ancient black kitchen range; pungent with hedgerow herbs and onions, it smelt appetizing. A battered old tom cat with a nicked left ear lay sociably by the fireside with a brindled lurcher, and Tansy was sprawled full-length on a prickly horsehair sofa clutching a fistful of steaming baked potato.

Zelda swept a pile of gaudy clothes from the back of an old wooden rocking-chair and asked me to sit down. Rowan, she said, was out ferreting and there was no telling when he would be back. Yes, Tansy could go to the village school if she wanted, she was only under her feet all day long getting into mischief. Yes, she could tell fortunes and would welcome the chance to earn a bit of money, as long as the council and the Inland Revenue didn't have to know; going round with their little books, sticking their noses into other people's business. The gypsies still lived like Stone Age hunter-gatherers and the authorities were not aware of their existence – that was how they liked it.

The child sulked when school was mentioned and took another bite of the hot potato, butter running down her chin. There were always plenty of vegetables to be got, a few lifted from a field here and there were never missed.

'Don't want to learn dusty old books,' she pouted.

'They go for walks in the woods,' I tempted her

'Picking blackberries and conkers?' she wanted to know.

'And conkers,' I agreed hesitantly, 'and you'll learn how to make apple dumplings.' She hurriedly gulped down a bite of potato.

'And wedding cakes?'

'When you're big enough.'

She decided she would give it a try and went round the room like a whirling dervish, kicking the animals who took no notice. I made a mental note to ask Kit to create another of his masterpieces – if we could get her to sit still long enough. His latest although not as accomplished as his landscapes, had a charm and a vitality of its own; the more you looked at it the more you liked it. He kept it hidden away for shame but said he would display it on Sunday. There was to be a Victorian Weekend in Haworth and some of the visitors would spill over into the surrounding countryside, but he didn't expect to sell anything.

'They come in out of the rain,' he complained, 'but don't buy.'

I arranged to pick Tansy up from school the next day and take her to Bobbin Yard for a sitting. One would be enough, Kit said, just to get the idea, and we spent a pleasant hour chatting on the cobbles.

Tansy wore a wizard's hat covered in wonky silver moons which she had made in class. She was a born actress and revelled in the limelight, tossing her head this way and that like a nervous Arab filly and seemed to be crestfallen when it was time to go home. All in all she had enjoyed her unusual day. An angry Rowan festooned with rabbits came to snatch her away and we had to warn him about the School Inspector.

'Get stuffed,' he said. 'I don't owe them anything.'

• • • • •

The whinook died down, the sun came out and lovers grappled each other against the trunks of ancient oaks. Myrtle gathered her green stuff from Hob Wood and cast some spells out of her witchcraft book from the public library. She flourished like the green bay tree and I felt like a dried-up river bed in comparison.

'Is she magic?' asked Julian. We agreed that she would never die but dissolve before our very eyes like Rider Haggard's *She*.

'It won't be long now,' she said mysteriously and when a letter came from the United States it was no surprise to her:

'Dear Ma'am,

I saw in the Georgetown Gazette that you are now in the tourist business. I shall be over in little old Yorkshire in June and intend to drop in on your little old homesteads of which I have fond memories. Tell me, is Myrtle Hawkweed still around there?

Yours respectfully,
Henry C. Waldorf'

Myrtle's high spirits brought on an attack of the doldrums in Otley. He lay in bed all day staring at the ceiling then rushed into my room wild-eyed.

'Let me go!' he shouted and made for the window as if to jump out. I shut it quickly.

'Go where?' I asked.

'Anywhere,' he said. 'Just to be free.'

'I thought you were going shark fishing,' I said.

'I shall only have to come back again.'

'No you won't if you don't want to.'

'Hard-faced bitch,' he glared. 'Care about nobody but yourself.'

I said if it was Nancy he wanted it was all right with me but to watch out for Billy Delph as he was after her as well.

'You're only jealous,' he said slamming the door as he went out.

Oh well, what shall I do next, I thought; unblock the drains or join the women's history class and learn how to be a person?

Kit was talking to the men working on the mill conversion. They were grouped artistically around the cement-mixer, their rippling muscles resting casually on their shovels. Perhaps they'd like some tea. I took out a tray and Kit said that he had sold Tansy and finished *Lady of the Lake* and would I like to see it. Standing in the beck with wet drapery clinging to her curves, Myrtle looked most uncomfortable: a long giraffe neck and hair like seaweed with a bird nesting in it; and what was that clutched in her right hand? It looked like a Cornish pasty – it was.

'What do you think?' he asked.

'Myrtle will love it,' I lied.

Kit came closer and it seemed there was an invisible thread spun secretly around us. My hands trembled and I let a mug slip from the tray on to the cobbles. We picked up the pieces of broken china cutting our fingers on the sharp slivers. Our blood mingled as we held hands.

'Now we are blood brothers,' he said.

I winced and wiped my hands on his painting smock.

'Help yourself,' he said.

The cement-mixer began to rumble and Judd Braithwaite advanced in a cloud of dust.

'We'll finish next week – that's if the lads can put in some overtime on Saturday to make up for last Monday.'

'What happened on Monday then?' I asked.

'They were on strike,' he said.

There is something about the word 'lads'. It conjures up a picture of blond Vikings on the rampage through Europe, raping and pillaging; or wild Mongol hordes sweeping across the steppes, bandy legs round the bellies of their little Mongol ponies.

The dust cleared. I looked across at the lads and got the impression that they had beat their swords into ploughshares for the time being only.

. . . . .

After spring-cleaning we brought all the Victorian knick-knacks into the parlour. Dusty aspidistras, stuffed birds, sea shells, Old Dobbins and Monarchs of the Glens, anti-macassars and glass ornaments with tinkling drops. All that red plush and tassels made it feel cosy at first but soon we had to rush out for air in case we choked.

'All this and gaslight as well,' said Freda. 'No wonder they died of consumption.'

Then we found some flannelette nightgowns, itchy combinations and frilly drawers. They suggested a warm, organic family life far removed from our own and I was loath to leave it until Freda picked up a leather belt with a heavy brass buckle on the end. Was it our imagination or was that a blood stain on it? The illusion of togetherness was gone.

'They were real families in those days,' said Otley, running his fingers along the mantelpiece to see how dusty it was. 'Can't you do anything properly?'

After leaving a mildewed copy of *Mrs Beeton* open casually at a recipe that needed a dozen eggs, a pint of cream and a bottle of sherry, we went down to the kitchen for our dinner.

'I'm starving hungry, what is it?' inquired Otley.

'Fish 'n' chips and mushy peas' I said.

'You know I don't like mushy peas,' he complained.

'Then don't eat them,' I said, devil-may-care.

'Are you a lesbian or something?' he wanted to know.

'Only sometimes,' I joked but he didn't laugh.

Freda and I thought the peas were a pretty shade of green but Julian thought there was too much E142 in them.

'Darren's mum makes him tandoori chicken,' he said, replacing the top on the ketchup bottle.

'Oh yes,' said Freda. 'And I expect he's got a real leather brief-case with his initials in solid gold.'

'Yes,' said Julian.

'And his father turns up on Sports Day with oranges and Mars bars for everybody.'

'How did you know?' he asked.

'Well why don't you go and live with Darren?' she sobbed.

'There's no room,' he said.

We washed the dishes and then switched on the box in time to see a film about jackals whose family life was an example to us all. It was Tom's birthday that week so, not wanting to be shown up by the jackals, I fetched my 'Come on Out' leaflets to see where we could go to celebrate. There was a Bouzouki Evening on at the Greek restaurant in Quarry Bottoms. Sounded all right to Tom.

'Sideways dancing and all that lark? Give up!' said Otley.

'A Ceilidh at the Shamrock Club?'

'I'm not Irish,' he said.

'A Highland Fling at the Temperance Hall?'

'I'm not Scotch,' he said with whisky in mind.

'Morris Dancing in the church hall?'

'I'm not English either – I'm Yorkshire.'

'Clog dancing then?'

'We haven't got any clogs,' he reminded us.

There was the *Revenge of the Nerds* on at the Picture House all this week, and you could get crisps and choc-ices there now, I reminded them.

'Take no notice, it's her age,' Otley advised.

In the end we decided to go walking with the Ancient Britons if the weather was fine. As it was Tom's birthday we would all go – it would be like Christmas but without the funny hats.

Noticing a blank space where Mike should have been, I went to see if he was in his room. There was no answer when I knocked so I looked through the keyhole but all I could see was a pile of old *Melody Makers*. I would have to write him a letter on manners like Lord Chesterfield used to do to his son. I began to compose it in my mind:

'Dear Boy,

> If I am rightly informed, I am writing to a fine young man in a new pair of Levis and Doc Martens, but I would remind you that men and women of discernment mind not the binding but the book. I much enjoyed your account of the workings of your wah-wah pedal and anxiously await your answers to the many questions I have asked you. Adieu.'

On second thoughts, if this sort of thing spread over twenty-eight years had no effect on the son of a noble lord, what chance did I have? I threw the letter in my mental dustbin.

NOT ONLY the air was balmy when we set out for Top Withens; we too were full of the joys of spring which had caught us unawares and upset our equilibrium. Sticky buds and furry catkins burgeoned forth and the melt-water sang its way down from the high moor into every nook and cranny. We leapt about like mountain goats until I got a splitting headache and Freda fell down a hole dislocating her kneecap. Tom, for his part, took the skin off his knuckles getting his hands trapped between two boulders while trying to emulate Joe Brown climbing the Old Man of Hoy. Nothing ever happened to Myrtle and Otley, only what they wanted to happen and they could be very scathing about other people's misfortunes. I should take feverfew for my migraines, Freda should look where she's going and Tom had seen enough rock-athletes on the box to know you had to have the right equipment. All of which was true but it didn't make us feel any better, especially as the Ancient Britons had jilted us too.

'It's like a Sunday School outing,' Otley said.

We reminded him of the times he had threatened to jump into the tarn, out of the window, off a skyscraper, in front of a bus, or had disappeared for hours while everybody frantically searched for him.

'That's different,' he said. 'I do it on purpose.'

We ate our sandwiches by the Brontë Bridge and reflected on the irony that we had only come for the good of our health. Our sandwiches were a bit squashed with the shaking they had undergone, and the tea had a head on it like a pint of bitter. We spread our plastic carriers on the damp earth and munched away as if there was no tomorrow.

Our personalities were well defined by what we chose to eat – Tom and Freda had cold roast-beef with lashings of mustard, and home-made apple pie with Wensleydale cheese; Myrtle had her salads and crispbreads and cottage cheese with pineapple. Otley tucked into salmon and cucumber rolls and a chunk of fruit-cake out of which he picked all the sultanas before he ate it, saying they looked like spiders; and I had triangular egg and watercress sandwiches and a slice of seed-cake. The seed-cake had been made by Miss Fidget, retired schoolmistress, and was once a favourite of Granny Hawkweed. Was I getting spinsterish in my old age? Otley looked across at me as I ate and I knew what he was thinking. Was I a lesbian, not eating the same as my husband like any normal woman?

Because of our injuries we had to abandon our walk to Top Withens, so we rested while Myrtle picked young hawthorn leaves to chew on, in order to prolong her lifespan. Otley consulted his map.

'I'm not sitting here like an old folks' home,' he said. 'I'll see if I can find the Pennine Way '

'Don't be too long,' we called after his vanishing bobble-hat.

We shifted restlessly as the cold struck through our plastic bags. For a time we amused ourselves by taking pain-killers and binding up our wounds, then Myrtle rose from Sladen Beck like Venus from the foam with a wet patch on her behind from sitting on the boulders.

'I'm cold,' she said. 'Let's go.'

Freda said she could walk slowly so we hobbled and staggered in the direction we had last seen Otley. The path took us past two derelict farms before meeting up with the Pennine Way, and we followed it down to Ponden. There was no sign of Otley so we stopped to look at the reservoir and then on to Ponden Hall – Thrushcross Grange in *Wuthering Heights*. The Pennine Way then took the high road up on to the moors and we parted company with it, Freda preferring to limp along the easy paths of the valley. There was still no sign of Otley and whenever we came to a reservoir we feared he might have flung himself into it.

Dr Moss called it 'nervous strain' but we often doubted that he had got it right.

'He was always disappearing when we were kids,' Freda said. 'If we went on an outing we spent all our time looking for him.'

It seemed he would go off with any stranger in preference to his own family and it was a miracle he had survived this long.

'And,' Freda continued, 'when mother asked him to switch the light off, he stood on his hands and put it off with his feet.'

He wanted to be different, he said, and who were we to say that he couldn't – but it did cause a lot of anxiety. Our culture, we thought that placed so much emphasis on freedom and individuality, had a lot to answer for.

He acted very peculiar at times, saying he was a werewolf and baying at the moon. Then there was the time he kicked me on the shins because I said that William the Conqueror was a Christian.

'He couldn't have been,' he protested.

'He was,' I said hopping on one leg, 'and so was Hitler.'

'And so was Jack the Ripper,' said Freda.

'Has everybody got God on their side?' Julian had asked.

We had to say yes because didn't the Bible say He loved sinners?

'Then why have we got to be good?' he went on.

We gave him another helping of pudding and changed the subject.

With a start we realized we had reached Watersheddles and were in Lancashire; we scanned the surface for a sign of Otley before turning back. We stopped to examine every dingle and dell and searched the horizon at frequent intervals like Stanley looking for Livingstone. Then we stopped for a ploughman's lunch before the pubs closed at three o'clock, resuming our search afterwards.

Myrtle turned defeat into victory by collecting greenery for her stuff and by now resembled a walking haystack. It was a nice afternoon so after scrutinizing Lower Laithe for a floating woolly hat we went where our fancy took us. To be honest, I was only going through the motions of looking for Otley. My worryometer had conked out long ago and he could have been fished out of the water and dumped at my feet lifeless. If the law allows you to kill in self-defence it will allow you not to worry on the same principle.

We had a cup of tea at Haworth, picked up some leaflets from the Information Centre then wandered down the cobbled Main Street to the bus stop; Myrtle couldn't get on the bus for foliage, so we shared it out among us. It would have broken her heart to leave it.

When we arrived home at last, weary and forlorn, we found Otley watching the six o'clock news and he wasn't very pleased.

'Where have you lot been to?' he demanded to know.

He said he had come back to where he had left us, and not finding us there he had taken the bus to Keighley and walked home from there. He was furious when we said we'd had a pub lunch and he refused to believe we had searched the reservoirs for him.

'Selfish lot,' he said. 'You only think about yourselves.'

The next day he packed up and went to Cornwall in a temper and we eventually received a postcard showing sixteen different kinds of fish that you can catch down there – only he hadn't caught any and it was the wrong time for shark fishing. There was a mizzle and he couldn't see the views, the landlady objected to him eating biscuits in bed and wouldn't let him hang his swimming trunks out of the window, so he was coming home.

What luxury it had been to be able to think without interruption, well almost. Myrtle took me in hand and practised her nature cures on me: herbal tonics and oatmeal baths, white of egg face-packs to iron out my wrinkles, lemon rinses for my hair and eyebright for my eyes. Then we looked through the Sunday supplements to see what the latest fashions were like and were astonished. The poor creatures looked like escaped lunatics with their grotesque posturing and multi-coloured layers of eccentric garments. We remembered when we were kids, running after gaudy, raucous jazz bands which were the highlight of our soberly-dressed year. Now everybody looks as if they're in a jazz band! We decided to stick to Marks & Spencer and the Co-op.

Then I had a lesson in wholefood cooking, which means making mud pies that you can eat. I must be honest and say that they tasted not at all bad. Pollen and ginseng and some stuff that was good for the libido Myrtle said, used his whole life long by a certain oriental sage who lived to be two hundred and thirty years old.

'But I don't want any libido,' I protested. 'I've only just got rid of it.'

'Don't you want to live as long as you can?' she asked.

'Only if I don't look like a two-hundred-and-thirty-year-old prune,' I pleaded to no avail.

Myrtle plastered my face and neck with Vitamin E anti-wrinkle moisturizer and assured me that if I used it morning and night for the rest of my life I would only look like a ninety-year-old prune.

'And don't forget to take these calcium tablets,' she warned. 'If your bones turn to jelly you won't be able to stand up.'

'Oh dear!' I said grabbing a handful and stuffing them into my mouth. I didn't want to get like poor old Aunt Adelaide who went wobbling about all over the place.

'You can get any man you want if you do yourself up a bit.'

'I don't want one,' I told her.

'I thought you fancied Kit.'

'I do, but . . .'

'But what?'

'It's all those wildlife documentaries,' I blurted out. 'If I see another rutting stag I'll put a brick through the telly.'

'I know,' she agreed. 'Ostriches and gadflies – they're all at it.'

'Last night,' I said, 'they told us the male frog will jump on anything that moves – it's the same with men.'

'The Bible says go forth and multiply,' Myrtle said as if that clinched it.

'I don't think it's meant to be taken literally, it says all sorts of things in the Bible,' I said hopefully. The Bible contains much wisdom as well as the conflicting statements that I could not fathom in a month of Sundays. I was a trial to Miss Robinson our Sunday School teacher. There was one black day in particular:

'Take your coat off,' she told me for the umpteenth time.

'I don't want to,' I said.

'God won't love you if you don't do as you're told,' she said.

'God doesn't know how cold it is in here,' I explained.

She seemed to froth at the mouth and threw her glove at me, catching me in the eye. I threw it back.

'God does not love wicked girls,' she said with one eye shut.

'It says here "eye for eye, tooth for tooth" in Exodus . . .'

She screamed with rage and locked me in the kitchen for the rest of the morning and I ate a box of jam tarts and currant buns left over from the Mothers' Meeting.

'It says "Turn the other cheek" as well,' she said when she let me out at dinner-time. 'Don't tell your mother, will you?'

I looked at the bit she was pointing to in St Matthew.

'How are we supposed to know what to do if they don't?' I asked.

'You are a very naughty little girl,' she told me shutting her Bible so that the dust flew out making us sneeze. 'I shall not mark your star card for today.'

It was a hot, sizzling Sunday so I cracked all the tar bubbles on the way home and got smacked for messing up my new shoes and socks. I got out my Bible to teach them a lesson.

'"Whoso shall offend one of these little ones which believe

in me, it were better for him that a millstone were hanged about his neck and that he were drowned in the depth of the sea!"' I read.

'Shut up!' they shouted and wouldn't let me have any pudding.

Grown-ups were funny, I thought, always preaching the Bible at you but they didn't like it if you preached it back.

So, all in all, I don't think God wanted us to go on multiplying until there wasn't an inch of space left on the globe. Myrtle made me take her libido pills all the same and asked me to get some more when I went shopping the next day. I looked at the list she put into my hand: magnetic insoles to massage her pressure points on the demos, Epsom salts to soak her feet in when she got back, lambswool to wrap round her bunions, slug pellets and a tin of tomato soup, a double toilet roll, either pink or white.

'And don't forget the passion pills,' she said.

It was a lovely morning and I enjoyed the walk down to the shop. I thought I caught a glimpse of somebody I knew but it was only me in the side window of the Co-op. I didn't recognize myself. Myrtle's stuff must be working: with my hair lightened and my weight going down I was passable again. I ran into trouble getting the toilet rolls; my request baffled the girl behind the counter.

'We haven't got any,' she said filing her nails.

I looked at the stacks of toilet rolls behind her.

'What are they then?' I inquired.

She flushed angrily and pointed her nail-file at me.

'You asked for pink or white, didn't you?'

'I did,' I had to agree.

'Well we've only got yellow or white.'

I could see she needed some help so I went behind the counter, picked a white one and held it up.

'Now I've got a yellow or white, haven't I?'

She burst into tears and fled, returning immediately with the manager. Customers were not allowed behind the counter and Miss Wakelin had threatened to leave if she got any more awkward trouble-makers. Who did I think I was? She'd had just about enough of it. I found myself apologizing like I do when somebody bumps into me, and hated myself for not wrapping the toilet rolls round their necks. I hid them inside my shopping bag and slunk out of the shop.

'Hello gorgeous, where have you been all my life?' said Kit, blocking my way. I racked my brains for a witty retort and failed to find one.

'Nowhere,' I said.

'You look smashing, you must be in love,' he said, his beard bristling. I looked up at the sky and said the clouds were a bit low down today and he said he thought they had been lower down yesterday. He showed me the painting he was taking to be framed. It was Jimmy One Eye and Percy Dredger sitting by the tarn in yellow oilskins and sou'westers and looking out over the water like *The Boyhood of Raleigh*.

'It's good,' I lied.

'I want to paint you someday,' he said.

'Whatever for?' I said, secretly flattered.

'You'd make a nice wood-nymph,' he said. 'Flowers in your hair and little cupids at your feet.'

'Where are you going to get cupids from round these parts?'

'I can imagine them – artistic licence,' he assured me.

'Then you can imagine a wood-nymph, can't you?'

I let myself be persuaded and we arranged to meet the next day in Hob Wood if the weather was fine.

• • • • •

I was up early the next morning in time to see a watery sun chase the moon out of the sky. There was a chill in the air so I put on a woolly vest and long johns under the sweet-pea chiffon which I borrowed from Myrtle, and took a wreath of wax orange-blossom out of one of the glass cases in the parlour for my head. It was the nearest I could get to *Primavera* but I had to spoil the effect by adding a plastic mac and green wellies.

'Shan't be long,' I said to Myrtle as she choked on her muesli. Kit was waiting at the gate and we took the path by the old railway into Hob Wood. Periwinkles spied on us with little blue eyes, and spikes of butterbur the colour of liver sausage, pushing up along the beck, looked startled to find themselves without their leaves. We found a silver birch that I could get my arms round if I fell down in the middle of a pose and I hid my boots and raincoat behind a boulder. I stood on one leg in a drift of wood anemones with my arm raised and looked fearfully over my shoulder as if I were running away from somebody.

'Can you just roll your trousers up a bit?' he said testily, as he added a bit of blue to the flesh pink he was mixing.

'They keep coming down,' I explained.

'Wood-nymphs don't have lumps,' he said, after I had rolled them up.

He threw a handful of celandines over me in gay abandon and started to paint. It was not possible to keep that position for long without getting cramp and I had to hold on to the tree.

'Imagine I'm not doing this,' I advised.

He kept holding up his brushes and looking at something with one eye shut, then he walked backwards and sideways and bent down to look under his easel.

'What's the matter, have you lost something?' I asked.

'I'm not entirely happy with the perspective,' he said. 'I'll leave the background unfinished as Leonardo did with the *Mona Lisa*.'

'Oh!' I said, smiling mysteriously.

'He used silk brushes though,' he said, adding some more blue. 'I'll have to make do with these nylon ones.'

After a while I collapsed into the anemones and we stopped for coffee and Marie biscuits. Kit picked some periwinkle leaves and handed me some to chew; they were a symbol of immortality he said. I washed mine in the beck first as a precaution against passing dogs. They tasted like poisoned cabbage as much as anything and I spat them out.

'Now you're mine for ever,' he said, looking into my eyes.

'How d'you mean?' I asked.

'Culpeper says, "Venus owns this herb and the leaves eaten by man and wife together cause love between them."'

'We're not man and wife.'

'Doesn't matter.'

I was losing my battle with Myrtle's stuff and when he came nearer I felt it would be nice to have a cuddle. I bubbled like a glass of hot champagne but in the end it was like kissing a box of Shredded Wheat and my head cleared.

'Have another biscuit,' I said, pouring out the rest of the coffee. 'And tell me, why do you want to cause love between us?'

'Why not?' he said with a Gallic shrug. 'Come over for a drink tonight and I'll play some records.'

'My husband's back tonight,' I told him. 'I'm on stand by.'

We walked out of the wood in silence, my wax orange-blossom digging into my forehead like a crown of thorns. The church clock struck one. Where had I been all morning, I asked myself in a daze, feeling like those people who set out on a twenty-minute drive home and arrive ten hours later, having been kidnapped by flying saucers. I let go of Kit's hand at the garden gate and left him looking like a thunderstorm.

'I hope we can still be friends,' I said amiably.

'Do you?' he replied.

OTLEY ARRIVED back from his holiday in a cloud of gloom. What a waste of time it had been. He felt worse now than when he went and that was the last holiday he would ever go on. But he had brought us all a present. A granite model of the Eddystone Lighthouse for me, a plate of rock ham and eggs for Mike, a pig with a daisy in its mouth for Myrtle, a tin of old-fashioned humbugs for Freda and Tom, and a 2,000-piece jigsaw puzzle of baked beans for Julian.

'That'll keep him quiet,' he said.

He left a trail of sand everywhere he went and when I asked him to clean it up he said that I was the hausfrau who wore a yellow wig so it was my job. Freda suggested we all go to Torremolinos and got out the brochure again; we would be sure to have a good time there.

'Too many foreigners,' said Otley, stretching out in front

of the telly. 'It's hard enough keeping your eye on them here.'

'I don't like the food,' Tom said. 'Just think what you'll get if you ask for fish fingers.'

'What?' Freda wanted to know.

'Octopus or something slimy like that,' he said.

Now I'm not mad on going abroad either but fair's fair and we eat some pretty revolting stuff here.

'Like tripe?' I asked.

'What's wrong with tripe?' he demanded.

'Well,' I said recklessly, 'when you see it draped over the counter like a pile of wet knitting, it's enough to put you off eating for life.'

'That's treason,' he said as I hung my head.

'What do you want with going abroad anyway?' Otley said. 'It's just as good down Boggle Clough.'

'Isn't that where your folks come from?' Freda asked as if it were ten thousand miles away.

'A very old family,' he nodded.

'How do you know if you've never traced them?' she asked as she handed out TV meals on plastic plates.

'I'm not wasting my time and money poking about in freezing cold churchyards getting pneumonia,' he said. 'It's not only royalty that's got a pedigree – I've got one too if I can find it.'

'How do you know?'

'How do you think I got here? I'm not a test-tube baby,' he said.

We had to agree that it was a bit much the way the top drawer went on about their ancient lineage, as if the rest of us had dropped out of a tree like rotten apples.

'I come from a long line of medieval oafs,' he said.

'Oh! Well that's different,' said Freda.

'And the only reason that they're up and I'm down is because my lot were getting the harvest in while they were slitting each other's throats for gold and putting their daughters up the duff.'

'If you feel that way,' I said, 'why are you always on the look-out for spies?'

'It's my hobby,' he said.

Having got that settled we watched a documentary about a man who spent his time opening barn owl pellets to see what they had been eating, followed by one about the CIA in El Salvador which put Otley in a good mood. It was the right time to ask him for the fifty pounds he had hidden away, so that I could buy a new coat. Oxfam was all right for a bit of fun but there came a time when you wanted a virgin. He said I looked fine in what I'd got but I explained that I didn't feel fine.

'Look,' he said. 'If I were a millionaire I'd buy you a mink.'

'I don't want a mink,' I assured him. 'I just want that fifty pounds in your pocket.'

'What fifty pounds?'

'In your top left-hand pocket.'

'Have you been spying on me again?' he asked.

'No,' I lied.

After threatening to steal a coat he said I could have the money but would I agree to a trial separation. He had had time to think while he was away and as we seemed to get on each other's nerves it might do us both good. He was serious about Nancy and he thought she felt the same way about him.

'I don't think so, she's been out with Billy Delph,' I told him, feeling like somebody who has just written a nasty letter signed 'Well-wisher'.

'You're jealous,' he said. 'And what were you doing in Hob Wood with Kit Constable?'

'Mind your own business.' How did he know so soon anyway? He raised his hand as if to strike me and I fled upstairs with him in pursuit.

'He's painting my portrait,' I said.

'In the woods?'

'I'm a wood-nymph.'

'You're getting senile in your old age,' he said.

'I've got as much right as you to be senile.'

'You're only trying to make me jealous,' he said.

'No I'm not.'

'Yes you are.'

We played at Punch and Judy for several minutes then he went to his room and came back with the money and a picture of the Bayeux Tapestry which he held under my nose.

'This money was for a telescope to look at Halley's Comet,' he said, pointing to the picture of King Harold getting it in the eye. 'It's here somewhere, if I can find it.'

His eyes were haunted and I almost weakened but that was the story of my life. I grabbed the money and made off with it.

'That's one in the eye for you then,' I said, locking my door.

'It won't be coming round again until the year 2061,' he shouted through the keyhole.

'Hard cheese,' I shouted back.

. . . . .

The lads made a good job of the conversion and went off to beat their swords into ploughshares somewhere else. But business was slow and our only customers were six people from a council home who went out licking ice cream cornets every day and came back drunk in a minibus at midnight. It gave us a chance to work on the details like whether our clientele would want to listen to 'Dirk Brooklime in Concert' with their hot buttered teacakes on a wet afternoon.

On the twenty-third of April we gathered round the stained-glass window on the landing to drink our health in nettle-beer. Ourselves first, Yorkshire second, then George and England a poor third. Then we pinned on our roses and wore them for the rest of the day – white ones of course. And although the Government have gone mad having May Day on the sixth we had ours at the proper time, dancing round the maypole on the first of May, with clog dancing in the church hall after a bun fight in the afternoon. Freda said we had run out of buns for the café so when I found a biscuit tin full of jam tarts I snatched it while Miss Fidget had her back turned and ran down the road with it under my coat. When I had put it away in the cupboard I was filled with remorse and knelt to say a prayer.

'God forgive me a miserable sinner,' I begged. 'You let Ronald Biggs get away, didn't you? Surely you don't begrudge us a few jam tarts.'

When I got back to the church hall Miss Fidget was looking puzzled. I gave her some tea and refrained from asking what was the matter. As the evening progressed the dancers complained of a nasty smell and we found Rowan sitting in a corner with two ferrets inside his shirt. He got belligerent when they danced past him holding their noses and pulled out his cut-throat razor.

'Anybody want to come outside?' he invited. Nobody did.

We thought it was a good time to put rabbit pie on the menu and said we were fed up with the poxy Chinese rabbits at the butchers. He took our orders and put his razor away.

'He could be useful in the patrol,' said Otley.

'I want nothing to do with the bluebottles,' said Rowan. 'I'm on my own.'

'It's not them, it's us,' Otley assured him.

'I want nothing to do with you either,' he said.

'Will you be on stand by?' Otley asked him.

'What's that?'

'To be called on in an emergency.'

'In a fight you mean?'

'Yes.'

'All right then – as long as I haven't to hang about like a line of wet washing.'

'Can I have your name, address and telephone number?' said Otley.

'Don't be so bloody stupid,' Rowan told him. 'You know very well I'm squatting in that mouldy old ruin. If you want me, throw a brick through the window – there's no glass in it.'

• • • • •

At a meeting under the Shire Oak it was agreed that for minor offences a spell in the stocks on market day would save the police a lot of bother. Half an hour for swearing, an hour for stealing food, two hours for money and three hours for causing an affray. All to be accompanied by rotten eggs and squashed tomatoes.

When Freda told me that Tansy was being blamed for taking the jam tarts I couldn't keep quiet any longer. It would mean disgracing my family but I couldn't let an innocent child suffer. I had to break the news to my husband and son first. How would they take it? Mike thought it was a huge joke and couldn't stop laughing. I reminded him sharply that his baseball boots wanted cleaning.

'What for?' he said. 'They'll only get dirty again.'

Otley was furious. I was showing him up again he said, he soon wouldn't be able to put his head out of the door.

'I thought we were having a trial separation anyway,' I said.

'I've changed my mind.'

He put on his best suit to take me to the council offices to see Billy Delph and make a confession. I stood in front of his desk tongue-tied.

'Go on then,' Otley nudged me. 'Tell him.'

I looked at Billy's massive shoulders, red-brown hair and eyes, and trembled as I thought of Farmer Bentley's bull.

'Well, it's like this,' I began, 'we were running short of buns at the café . . .'

'Oh! I can't worry about things like that,' Billy interrupted. 'I'm short of pig's trotters but I don't go round telling everybody.'

'You don't understand,' I told him. 'I took the jam tarts from the church hall – it wasn't Tansy.'

'And letting the kids get the blame for it,' he said. 'Aren't you ashamed of yourself?'

'Yes,' I lied. The tarts had gone down a treat and the money was safely in the bank now.

'Well,' he said, picking up his meat cleaver,' I won't chop your hand off this time, but you'll have to go in the stocks; can't make any exceptions.'

'Yes Mr Delph,' I said hanging my head.

'Make an example of her,' said Otley.

'And make some more tarts for Miss Fidget,' said Billy.

'I will,' I said as if I were getting married.

Luckily it was sunny on the Saturday so I put my swimming costume on under a red shower-proof anorak and trousers and Otley took me by the shoulder and marched me off. I had to face my ordeal alone as Freda was doing some washing and Myrtle had gone into Keighley shopping. They always stared at her as if she had gone mad when she asked for quark at the local Co-op. My husband was too ashamed of me to give me moral support and he went back home saying that Granny Hawkweed would be turning in her grave.

A little group gathered and somebody said I must have had a brainstorm doing things like that. If you're going to show yourself up like that, it might as well be for a million-pound bank robbery as for a box of jam tarts. That's true, I thought, I'll bear that in mind for next time.

Some tut-tutted saying we had gone back to the barbarous Middle Ages and tried to cheer me up.

'Did you get your shoes from Woolworth's? They are nice!'

'Would you like a drink of water?'

'What a fuss over a few jam tarts!'

Some urchins ran past throwing squashed tomatoes they had found in the boxes behind the market stalls, and their aim was deadly, giving me a free face-pack. I spat out the pips like Nell Gwynne.

'I expect they're from that new council estate,' said Granny Blinks, chasing after them with her umbrella. Somebody else kindly offered me an after-dinner mint which I chewed while Billy Delph publicly admonished me and then decided to let me out.

It wasn't too bad. I was among friends and I went home with the crowd following me to the garden gate where I waved them goodbye. When they had gone I found some dock leaves and brushed the debris from my hair and clothing before going indoors to be welcomed by my loving husband.

'Don't come here in that state,' Otley said. 'Go and have a bath first!'

'I'm going to,' I said agreeably.

When I emerged clean and respectable again he offered to fetch some fish and chips for the four of us, Myrtle being back and Mike having materialized like the penguins at feeding time in the zoo.

'What skinny little pieces of fish,' Otley complained as he unwrapped the greasy bundles. 'You can catch bigger ones than that in Ousel Beck.'

IT WAS nearly midsummer and while the rest of us were busy piling up sticky buns into something resembling a Common Market food mountain, Nancy was to be seen getting into Billy Delph's peppermint Peugeot and driving off into the countryside.

'Well, he's got rump steak for the asking,' said Tom.

But Otley could not accept that bow-legged Billy, who couldn't stop a pig in a ginnel, was preferable to his handsome good self.

'I've had enough,' he cried. 'I'm going to jump in the tarn!'

He put his jacket on and made for the door. I beat him there and spreadeagled myself in front of it. He pushed me aside.

'Jezebel!'

'Don't,' I begged. 'You can have anything you want. You can have my Polaroid sunglasses – when we get some sun.'

'I've done my best – haven't I been a good husband?'

'Yes,' I said. 'Well, most of the time.'

'Nobody cares about me!'

'We do, we do,' I assured him. 'You can have my Parker pen and my index-linked National Savings Certificates.'

He curled his lip and took his jacket off again.

'Besides,' said Freda, 'they might only be going to the cemetery with flowers for his wife.'

For the next few days, while the less sensitive of us got on with the work, Otley stayed in bed and had his meals on a tray. I thought I would be kind to him and give him a kiss with his boiled egg one morning; he held up an unshaven chin.

'Come on then and be quick about it – there's *Gardeners' Question Time* on Radio Four.'

'I didn't know you were interested in gardening,' I said. 'You never do any.'

'I'm interested in proper gardens, not that cat-run we've got round the back.'

I suggested going to the Great Yorkshire Show this year but he said it was too much to take in. He didn't like big things. Chelsea Flower Show, national garden festivals, grandiose stately homes, royal variety shows with a cast of thousands and a turn a minute. They can all get stuffed. What did he want then?

'You said I could have anything I wanted, didn't you?'

'I did,' I said with some regret.

'We'll have a survival weekend up on the moors. All of us. We need to battle with the elements, toughen ourselves up.'

'What for?'

'What do you think the Yanks and Russians are coming here for? A one-eyed hole like this. There's something afoot.'

'They're coming to see where the Brontës lived.'

'Give up! you don't think they're bothered about *Jane Eyre* do you? There's something fishy going on.'

I said I'd see what the others thought about it. His eyes had a glazed look.

'In 1944, September seventeenth . . .' he began and then stopped. I held my breath hoping he would go on. Mike had often asked what he had done in the war but it remained a mystery. It must have been something nasty to be hidden away in a metal box under the floorboards, and he watched over it like the dragon guarding the golden fleece. What could it be? There were endless permutations, it was better than the football pools. Did he punch the Commanding Officer? Get drunk and give away all the parachutes for making into camiknickers? Did he let his gun go rusty or set the NAAFI on fire? We had resigned ourselves to never knowing the truth, perhaps it was for the best.

'Tell them I shall throw myself in the tarn if they won't go,' he said, turning his eggshell upside-down and smashing it with his spoon.

'It's a small thing to ask,' said Dr Moss when I telephoned him later. 'Lots of people do that and they're not suffering from nervous strain.'

'It's not that,' I told him. 'He's been in bed for four days and he won't get up.'

'He'll get up when you go camping. Don't make a mountain out of a molehill Mrs Craven. If you call in I'll give him some different tablets.'

I went across to Bobbin Yard that evening to see my portrait. It was a very lumpy wood-nymph that looked back at me, with a face like a wax doll melting in the sun and a silver birch growing out of her head.

'What do you think?' he asked me.

'The silver birch is good,' I said truthfully, ignoring the rest of it.

'Mind you,' he said, 'I like those fat Rubens women – plenty to get hold of.' He gave me an old-fashioned look and I made a mental note to get back on my diet. We looked at a book about the French Impressionists and listened to some sparkling music to match and so passed a pleasant hour until he reached out over the marmalade cat to grab hold of me. I hit him with *Painting for Beginners* and fled into the night. Otley was up now. He was watching the German film *Das Boot* with Myrtle and Mike.

'Where have you been to?' he demanded when I crept in.

'Out,' I said.

All eyes turned back to the small screen. It was a taut, tense film with electronic music that sounded like the ticking of the doomsday clock. Myrtle and I cried at the end when the poor Germans and their submarine got blown up.

'You're only supposed to cry for your own side,' Otley said.

'They made me a European when I didn't want to be one,' I told him, 'so now they can take the consequences.'

'And they've got the cheek to tell us to buy British,' said Mike picking up his Sony Walkman. 'Good night.'

'Good night,' we said in a Greek chorus.

Otley was now engrossed in a documentary about Haiti and the Tonton Macoute and answered irritably when I inquired after his health.

'Of course I'm all right, don't nanny me!'

I had lit the blue touch-paper again, so there was nothing to do but retire. As I passed the stained-glass window the new moon sat sideways on St George's head, making him look like a Viking with a horned helmet and for some reason I found myself wondering what the lads were up to.

The clang of Heavy Metal issued from Mike's room and I couldn't help thinking that Otley was right when he said the younger generation would be deaf before they were forty. Mike had refused our invitation to go on a survival weekend.

'You're a pampered lot!' Otley told him. 'God help us if we get invaded; you'll have to play them to death!'

Perhaps I could get him to change his mind. I knocked on the door. No answer so I shouted through the keyhole.

'Rehearsals going all right?'

'Yes.'

'How's Dirk these days?'

'All right.'

'And how's Mrs Brooklime?'

'All right I expect.'

'Everything O K at school?'

'No.'

'Why, what's wrong?'

'Nothing.'

'Here's five pounds for some new strings and plectrums,' I lied. The door opened and a smiling face appeared to say its thanks.

'It would be nice if you'd come with us. Your father's got a book *Survival for Young People* especially for you.'

'It's a waste of time, there'll be no survivors if there's another war.'

'It's as well to be prepared – like the Boy Scouts,' I reminded him hopefully, but thinking at the same time how silly it sounded.

'What's the use of rubbing two sticks together to make a fire if you've got no skin?'

While I was thinking of an answer to that he was gone and I faced a locked door again. There seemed to be no way of getting through to this punk generation and I was beginning to feel sorry for their teachers. I would have to write him a letter:

'Dear Boy,

> If I am rightly informed, I am writing to a fine young man in a new pair of mercerized cotton socks Made in China. I much enjoyed your account of the workings of your Sony Walkman, with its anti-rolling mechanism, three-band graphic equalizer and Dolby B noise reduction and I anxiously await your answers to the questions I have asked you. Adieu.'

But this was not the House of Commons and even written questions went unanswered so I decided to write out the Co-op groceries instead.

. . . . .

Our survival weekend nearly killed us. It was blowing a gale and we spent most of the time struggling with a box of soggy matches. Sticks were washed away and it was no use chasing them to rub them together to make a fire. We ate cold baked beans and drank cold tea and huddled together in the tent for warmth, but only succeeded in making each other wetter.

'We shall all get pneumonia,' said Freda.

'Ging-gang-gooly,' Otley sang merrily.

We stuck it out until nearly Sunday dinner-time when we started to dream about Yorkshire pudding and decided to go home.

'We've gone soft,' Otley grumbled. 'I don't know what Hank Waldorf will think. Did you see *Rawhide* – living for months on coffee and beans and fresh air?'

'This is more fresh water,' observed Tom.

'It's good for the complexion,' said Myrtle catching some in an empty baked-bean tin. Hank was expected any time now as he wanted to be at the Midsummer Feast the following day. We had learned too that the Soviet Trade Delegation would like to see something of our quaint customs. With a bit of luck we had time to get home and make ourselves respectable, so we packed up our drowning equipment and, driven hither and thither by the raging whinook which was fortunately blowing our way, we galloped over the moor like demented pack-mules.

'The exercise'll do you good,' said Otley encouragingly as I caught my foot in a rabbit-hole and fell flat on my face.

There was a buzz of excitement as we reached the village green and a small crowd had gathered round a strange car that grinned at us like a Japanese general. A fat John Wayne leaned on it chewing.

'That can't be him,' Myrtle said. 'He was like Henry Fonda.'

He swaggered towards us wearing a yellow shirt with multi-coloured views of London, Paris and New York, a Nikon round his neck and a bulging wallet in his hand.

'Flash git,' said Otley.

'Myrtle Hawkweed!' the stranger exclaimed, grabbing her in a bear-hug. 'You haven't changed one li'l bit.'

'Nice to see you,' said Myrtle flatly as she untangled her hair from his camera straps.

'It's great to be back in wet and windy ol' Yorkshire,' Hank said. 'Say! you guys look like you bin dredged up from the bottom of the Atlantic Ocean.'

'We've been camping,' I said.

'In this weather?'

'It's going to be sunny tomorrow,' said Freda taking off her dripping anorak. 'It's clearing up now.'

We all looked up at the black cloud rolling away from us and wondered if it would be coming back again.

'I'll say this, you sure are ready for anything,' Hank went on. 'It's a smart cookie who can put anything over on you guys.'

'Yabba dabba doo!' cried Otley as he bounded off down the road.

'GEE THIS is kinda cute,' said Hank as we showed him to the flat at the top of the old mill. He kept ducking his head as if he expected to be decapitated at any minute, and changed his loping strides into small, shuffling ones that made him look like an overgrown geisha. Freda made some coffee in her fitted kitchen with the split-level cooker, and we sat round a white formica table like medical students waiting for an operation. Hank left most of his coffee and Julian felt he had to apologize.

'They're all right at making tea and cheese sandwiches but that's about all.'

Hank guessed he didn't come here for the food or he would have gone to France or Italy, and he'd noticed there were several Chinese takeaways round about, not to mention Wimpys and Taj Mahals.

'There's a Cordon Bleu class at the Tech. but they won't go,' Julian complained. 'It's never too late to learn.'

'There's no call for that sort of thing round these parts,' said Freda. 'Who's going to eat it?'

'You see what I'm up against,' Julian appealed to Hank. 'They think because they're older than me they're more intelligent.'

'The older you get the sillier you get,' said Hank giving Julian's hair a friendly ruffle.

'They've always been like that,' Julian told him.

'Like what?'

'Brooke Bond's chimpanzees.'

'Have you done your homework yet?' Freda inquired.

'Yes.'

'Oh!' she said nonplussed. 'Well – have a piece of slab cake.'

Myrtle seemed to go down like a flat tyre when Hank brought out his family photographs. He had been married three times and had five children and twelve grandchildren. There was a Southern Belle with fat, blonde curls tied back with a fat magnolia blossom.

'This here's ma first wife Prissy, ran off with a member of the Ku Klux Klan.'

A Southern Belle with black ringlets, drinking a mint-julep, was his little Marilou who met a tragic end.

'Fell overboard in the Everglades and got eaten by 'gators.'

Then there was Betsy Ann, the schoolmarm, who had made life so unpleasant that he took to playing truant from his marriage and was eventually expelled. A flurry of snapshots followed.

'And this here's Gaylord, Lelord, Beauregard, Georgina and Lulubelle – and here's ma grandchildren, Fontaine, Marietta, Lee, Daisybelle, Charlotte . . .'

'Would you like some tea?' I interrupted. Myrtle looked grim as she helped me get it ready.

'But I never forgot my li'l ol' Yorkshire Rose,' he called.

'He had a jolly good try,' she muttered, her eyes blazing like a wild-cat's. The next day she tore up the yellowing photograph of Hank in his flying jacket and gave 'Carolina Moon' to the Boy Scouts to be melted down and made into a flowerpot.

'He hasn't come here to see me,' she said. Otley knew why he was here and told us all over again.

'There's something fishy – him and the Russians being here at the same time; it's the KGB and the CIA.'

'Let's keep politics out of it,' I implored. 'It's the Midsummer Feast tonight, be off duty for once.'

'They're never off duty are they?'

'They're only here for a few days, don't spoil it.'

He seemed to be searching frantically for something and ignored my request.

'Have you seen my silk shirt with the pink stripes – I can't find it anywhere?'

'I expect it's in the wash,' I told him and his face took on the same expression as when I said that William the Conqueror was a Christian.

'You'll wash it to smithereens one of these days,' he said.

• • • • •

In our anxiety to make our Russian guests feel at home we had been struggling with an old Russian phrase-book that we got for ten pence at a jumble sale. Some pages were missing, others were scribbled on but we managed to learn a few things like 'I resign', 'My ear hurts' and 'Have you any ladies' vests and pants in pale blue?' We skipped over the difficult ones like 'He is making experiments in ultra-long-distance television reception' and others such as 'Have you any breeches?' and 'Where is my whip?' which seemed to have a somewhat sinister aspect.

'They all speak English anyway,' Otley said. 'They learn it in their spy schools.'

Ivan arrived alone on a motorbike and was not at all what we expected. A tall, blond Lithuanian from the Amber Coast, he unfurled himself from his machine and came to meet us with outstretched arms. For a moment there was stunned silence, then Freda rushed forward to take his hand.

'My ear hurts,' she said in confusion.

'Heallyo,' he said in a voice from *Boris Godunov*. Was he going to sing for us?

We showed him to a flat as far away from Hank as possible, in case they took it into their heads to liquidate each other in the dead of night, and then made some tea. When Ivan asked for a slice of lemon and a spoonful of honey Myrtle questioned him further. Yes, he ate yoghurt and sunflower seeds, black bread and a salad every day. He was a teacher of physical education in Kaunas and was with the Soviet Trade Delegation as an observer.

'Observing what?' Otley wanted to know.

'Your dyemyocryacyi.'

'Liar,' Otley mouthed behind Ivan's back.

We showed our guests round the village but Ivan was more interested in Marks & Spencer than Karl Marx.

'I get djeanz,' he said holding up his leg. Myrtle said she would get them for him and they gazed into each other's eyes. Hank had gone quiet for an American, so I took his arm in sympathy and pointed out the Primitive Methodist Chapel and Granny Blinks's Old Curiosity Shop. Just then Nancy emerged in a tight red skirt and a frothy blouse. She teetered up to us on stiletto heels, lips raspberry-red like a child caught in the jam-pot.

'Hi,' she said, giving Hank an appraising look. 'If it isn't Robert Redford himself.'

'What's a cute li'l girl like you doin' in a one-horse town like this?' he said, his camera ready for action.

'I live here.'

'Say cheese.'

'Gorgonzola,' Nancy said and they both fell about laughing.

'How about a coming for a drink?' Hank suggested.

'It's not opening time yet,' we reminded him.

'I'd forgotten,' said Hank. 'You can only feed when the keeper opens the gates.'

'Is that your car?' asked Nancy, her eyes lighting up with dollar signs.

'Sure, who else would have an automobile like that,' said Hank, and he was right.

. . . . .

'I'll never let you go!' Otley said when we got back.

'I'm not going anywhere,' I told him.

'I saw you holding his arm,' he said as he examined his teeth in a magnifying mirror.

'We're just good friends,' I said flippantly. He made a move as if he was going to strangle me then changed his mind.

'I'll have to get some gold fillings,' he said, going back to his teeth. 'These mercury ones are poisoning me.'

Mike came in and said Nancy had gone off with Hank in his car in the direction of Skartha, and Julian heard him on the phone arranging to meet somebody in Ilkley. He had put the phone down when he saw Julian, saying 'Little pitchers have big ears.'

'I'll inform the Watch,' said Otley.

'Why would they be spying round here?' I asked, handing him a cup of hot milk for his nerves. 'There's only derelict mills.'

'I know how they work,' he said. 'They pick places like this for dead-letter drops.'

'And I bet that's a James Bond car he's got.'

'All right Mrs Know-all,' he snapped.

I really must put some zip into his life, I thought, but nothing was going to make me look like Cleopatra however hard I tried. Then I suddenly remembered the Indian squaw outfit in the lumber room. Myrtle had been Pocahontas in the school pageant and had treasured the costume ever since. It might be a bit on the tight side for me but I expect there are fat squaws as well as thin ones, and it would be a change from the *Sound of Music* stuff.

'She's gone off with that Ivan the Terrible on his motor-bike,' Freda said as we helped to dismantle the Common Market Sticky Bun Mountain to take up to Druid's Altar.

'She'll tell him anything he wants to know,' said Otley.

'She'll get kidnapped by White Slavers and end up in Beirut,' Freda said. 'We'll all be murdered in our beds.'

'They said they'd be back by six o'clock,' said Julian. 'They've only gone to Marks & Spencer's.'

'A likely story,' said Otley, getting out his maps. 'Which way did they go?'

'Down Boggle Road to Keighley,' said Julian.

'That's just to throw us off the scent,' Otley said. 'I expect they doubled back and went over the moor to Skartha.'

There was work to be done and some of us haven't got the time to be spies so we had to leave him to it. Mike came down with some dirty washing as a present for me, a Union Jack pants and vest. He gave me a pat and asked if there was anything he could do to help. Now what is he after, I wondered – another wah-wah pedal? And those pants! I would have to write him a letter.

'Dear Boy,' I would have to say, 'It has come to my attention . . .' but what's the use? He would only make paper darts with it.

'You don't know what you're letting yourself in for,' Myrtle said as I squeezed into the fringed buckskin and adjusted my feather.

'How do you mean?' I said, sticking on false eyelashes.

'The men,' she explained. 'They'll be like wasps around a jam-pot. I had to climb out of the window and run all the way home.'

'You were only sweet sixteen, nobody's going to swarm round me at my age,' I assured her.

'The old 'uns will,' she said, twisting daisy-chains into her corrugated hair.

'They'll all be after Nancy anyway.'

'Not when they see a Red Indian – it's all those cowboy films – it causes a stampede.'

It was a bright, starlit night so we walked up Ridings Fell in an unruly procession. The Watch went first, carrying their makeshift weapons. Billy with his cleaver, Percy with a dipstick, Jimmy One Eye with a pitchfork and Otley with a wooden meat tenderizer snatched from the kitchen as we went through.

'Rowan said he'd bring his cut-throat razor,' he confided.

The lasses carried summer nosegays, the lads transistors and a medley of weird noises filled the air. Mike had been bribed into bringing some 'Hey Nonny No' music for us Ancient Britons, and Stalin had a piglet on a chain that was giving us all meningitis with its squealing.

'I couldn't leave him,' he explained. 'His mother will sit on him and squash him.'

Old Abel Earnshaw came out and cursed us for heathens saying he hoped Halley's Comet came and gave us the plague.

'It's John the Baptist's birthday,' shouted Otley. 'Ignorant git.'

'Who's that?' Hank asked, nodding in my direction. Nancy drew his attention to the stars and held his arm in a vice-like grip.

'It's a night for romance,' she said, breathless in her tight-laced, Nell Gwynne bodice.

We tripped up the fell like merry trolls bent on a night of mischief, chattering away like thieving magpies, except for Julian.

'Stupid lot!' he said. 'I hope they're not going to sing.'

He had inherited this aversion to singing from Granny Hawkweed who detested the orgies of community singing on the sea front at Blackpool. As a child she would stand with head bowed and tears streaming down her cheeks while the crowd sang 'Goodbye Dolly I Must Leave You', and at birthday parties she would plead with her mother beforehand, 'You're not going to sing are you?' and sit under the table with her fingers in her ears until they stopped.

So Julian had brought his rubber ear-plugs that he wore when he went swimming and a pound of potatoes to bake on the fire. Uncle Otley had his metal-detector so that when they got fed up they could go and look for pirate's gold.

'Yindyians!' Ivan said to Myrtle as he followed my tracks.

'It's only May,' she said leading him away with a sesame crunch.

It was a hard climb up the hill and we stopped to rest and admire the view. All around was bathed in silver moonlight, like one of Emily Brontë's poems. No wonder they had spent so much time up on the moors.

'If they'd gone the other way they'd have been knee-deep in sewage,' said Otley, his face lantern-lit like a Rembrandt.

'I'm hungry,' said Julian. 'Can I have a samwidge?'

'We're not there yet,' Freda told him.

'I know that but can I have a samwidge?'

'He's like a waste-disposal unit,' complained Tom.

We reached the stone circle by midnight and Miss Fidget had set out a buffet on Druid's Altar which made a good picnic table. Being the one who was teetotal she was in charge of the beer and wore her Cub mistress uniform to discourage skylarking.

'Hello gorgeous!' said Kit suddenly appearing from behind a boulder. 'I didn't know it was you – you look different.'

'It's a change from twin sets and pearls,' I said, twiddling my plaits nervously.

'I'll say it is.' The gleam in his eye and the wolf-whistles I was getting made me think that Myrtle was right. I found myself wishing I had brought a tomahawk.

• • • • •

The fire was soon roaring away and we stood looking at it for a bit then Miss Fidget poured out ginger-beer and elderberry wine into paper cups. Stalin's pig broke loose and got under everybody's feet squealing blue murder.

'That pig's going to get roasted in a minute,' Tom said.

Mike flung himself on it and flattened it then tied it to a tree and came back to play some tapes. We had the 'Merry Maidens' first in which the lads carried them off at the end, and as the lads included our Vikings from the building site we couldn't be sure whether they would bring them back again.

'Keep your eye on them,' Otley said to Billy Delph.

Then we sang 'There is a Tavern in the Town' and 'I'm Off with the Raggle-taggle Gypsies-O' and Otley took Julian off metal-detecting.

Hank sang 'I Was Born under a Wandering Star' and then came over to sit with me. Nancy followed.

'Hiya honey,' he said. 'You squaw, me squaw-man.'

'Hello Mr Waldorf,' I said primly. 'I think it's going to rain.'

'Been doin' a rain-dance have you?'

'There's no call for them here,' I said.

'Relax,' he told me. 'Big Chief Sitting Bull gone hunting.'

He put a large arm around me as I poked in the fire with a stick to see if the potatoes were done. Nancy was not at all pleased. After a while she got tired of sitting there in silence with us like the Three Wise Monkeys and tried to lure him away on a guided walk. He didn't want to go.

'Squaw take squaw-man back to wigwam,' he suggested. Nancy lost her temper at this and grabbed a piece of rope off Stalin.

'Squaw-man get lynched,' she threatened and he went.

We sang 'All by Yourself in the Moonlight' and did a conga round the stone circle; Aunt Janey sprained her ankle and held her nose as Stalin carried her back to the bonfire and bound it up with his red spotted handkerchief.

'I hope you've washed it,' she said.

As the night went on the music changed to the top ten and white punk faces appeared out of the dark, like spirits of the dead at a corroboree. We thought we recognized one.

'Isn't that Susan Mitchell?' said Freda.

'The one with the green and purple hair?'

'No, she's got a red spike on top and a silver spike at each side, like Boadicea's chariot.'

'In the lace dress and moon-boots, with a safety pin through her nose?'

'That's her,' said Freda.

We gave them some ginger-beer and a sticky bun and they began to jump up and down to the music like on *Top of the Pops*, but we had to draw the line when Clint Sidebottom tried to spin round on his head on the top of Druid's Altar.

'You'll get a splitting headache,' we told him.

'See you later darling,' Kit called out to me as he danced by with Miss Fidget.

'She's a fine figure of a woman in her Boy Scout uniform,' said Billy Delph who had gone off tight skirts and frothy blouses.

We whirled in a giddy circle round the bonfire, representing the planets orbiting the sun, but Mr and Mrs Brooklime and Floradora clasped each other and danced as they lived, in an eternal triangle.

Myrtle and Ivan stood in the glow of the fire like Tristan and Isolde; they seemed happy to be sharing their bamboo shoots like a pair of mating pandas. Then suddenly he was at my side.

'Yindyian Lyov Call,' he announced. Was he going to sing it?

I poked about in the fire with my stick, picking out the baked potatoes. I handed him one and it burnt his fingers. Myrtle's look said 'I told you so' and when he asked for some Indian medicine she said she had a tube of calendula ointment somewhere if he would help her to find it.

The music faded away as the merry-makers flopped to the ground like rag dolls. There was no singing now so Otley and Julian returned from treasure hunting with some brass buttons off a blazer which they had hoped were Roman coins.

'You might as well be dead,' he said.

'Never mind, you might find some tomorrow,' I told him.

'Good God! What are you doing dressed up like that?' he asked.

'Miss Armitage says . . .' I began.

'Sod Miss Armitage – getting people to make bloody fools of themselves.'

'It's a change,' I said, adjusting my drooping feather.

'I've enough on as it is coping with myself without being saddled with a wife like you.'

'How do you mean?'

'You're a nymphomaniac, after every Tom, Dick and Harry.'

'What's a nymphomaniac?' Julian wanted to know.

'An enthusiastic young dragon-fly,' I lied.

'No it isn't,' he said.

'If you know why did you ask?'

'I've had enough, I'm going home,' Otley said, packing up his metal-detector. 'What's that Russian up to I'd like to know.'

'You have to leap over the fire first or you'll turn into a frog,' we warned him. One after another we jumped over it leaving behind a smell of scorched rubber.

'If I'm going to turn into a frog I might as well go and jump in the tarn,' he cried as he ran off into the night. We called him back but the rocks bounced our voices to and fro like a ping-pong ball. We wondered if we would ever see him again.

Aunt Janey was pleased when Stalin's pig went missing and stifled a laugh when he sobbed.

'He was there asleep wi' his little tail curled up.'

Somebody said they saw the gypsy from Bilberry Cottage lurking about but somebody always says that so we took no notice. Julian singed his hair rummaging for potatoes and gave Freda the fright of her life.

'You worry me to death,' she scolded. 'I shall look like an old witch by the time you've grown up.'

'You look like an old witch now,' he said frankly.

'I'd give him a leathering if he were mine,' said Stalin.

'I expect you would,' sniffed Aunt Janey. 'You're only used to pigs that grunt.'

Billy Delph came back holding Rowan by the scruff of the neck. He had been caught with the pig under his arm like 'Tom, Tom the Piper's Son'. Its chops were tied up to stop it squealing.

'Poor little George,' said Stalin. 'He's worse than your mother.'

Rowan pleaded that he'd had a deprived childhood with no toys, his wife had taunted his manhood and the police were picking on him.

'It's nothing to do with the police,' said Billy. 'I'm the boss here; you'll have to go in the stocks.'

'In front of everybody?' said Rowan.

'Don't think you can do what you like just because you're a gypsy,' Billy told him. 'We treat everybody as bad as each other.'

'How long for?' asked Rowan anxiously.

'An hour for stealing food.'

'You'll never get a council house now,' Freda said.

'I don't want a bloody council house.'

'Good job too,' we said.

• • • • •

We made our way home through the dark conifer woods and out into the bright moonlight, the moors hunched all around like sleeping dinosaurs. I stopped when we came to the tarn and wondered if Otley had flung himself into its silent depths or if he had gone home. From past experience I knew it would be the latter yet I couldn't bring myself to pass it. I hung back until the others had gone and then sat staring at the water. Presently there was a scrambling noise on the rocks behind and I started as Kit's voice rang out shattering the silence.

> 'By the shore of Gitche Gumee,
> By the shining Big-Sea-Water.'

He said he had been waiting to catch me alone all night and why was I playing hard to get. He moved closer, his beard tickled my neck and I felt a shiver go down my spine. I looked at the sky.

'Have you ever painted silver moonlight?' I asked.

'I'm not here to talk shop,' he said, flinging himself at me with such force that my wampum gave way under the strain. Myrtle's libido pills took over and my head swam, making the stars above spin round like a catherine wheel. Then, as in all the Westerns, the cavalry came to the rescue, just in the nick of time.

'Geronimo-o-o!' yelled Otley as he came leaping over the rocks. There were a few punches thrown and I felt ridiculous, like a half-chewed ham-bone with two dogs scrapping over it.

'That's my wife don't forget,' Otley reminded Kit.

'No hard feelings old chap,' said Kit. 'You know how it is.'

They shook hands and agreed that I did look fetching dressed like Minnehaha; it was no wonder men lost their heads when women led them on. I maintained an embarrassed silence all the way home.

'Don't worry,' Otley shouted through my locked door. 'I don't want you – I'm not letting anybody else have you, that's all.'

MIKE'S MUSIC woke me at midday with a noise like the sound of dustbins being emptied. Couldn't he play something pretty – like fairy-bells tinkling? I asked him through the keyhole; something you can sing to.

'You can't sing,' he said.

'That's true,' I had to admit.

I took Pocahontas back to the lumber room and put her to sleep for another generation, wondering what it was about her that encouraged middle-aged men to lose their marbles. Myrtle had taken Ivan to Haworth and I faced Otley over the beans on toast like a war-weary general ready to sue for peace.

'Lovely day isn't it?' I said, looking out of the window.

'No it isn't.'

'Sorry about last night,' I lied.

'You get sillier as you get older.'

'You said that yesterday,' I reminded him.

'My molecules are all shook up,' he complained. 'You've got no consideration.'

'We were only talking.'

'In body language – like the naked ape,' he said.

'Have a cup of tea,' I soothed.

'You're not like a proper wife,' he said.

'How do you mean?'

'Knitting socks, making treacle pudding, You're always reading; it's not normal.' I wondered how it was that I had to be normal while he was as mad as a hatter.

'Miss Armitage wants to see us again,' I said.

'Stuff Miss Armitage!'

Anyway, I pointed out, it was Tom who liked treacle pudding not him but he said there was a principle at stake.

'And Kirk Douglas's wife runs to meet him with a drink every time he comes in,' he said, savaging his toast.

'So would I if I were Kirk Douglas's wife,' I said rashly.

If Myrtle had not returned at that moment he would have strangled me with the oven gloves; as it was he just kicked me on the shins under the table.

'*Dossvidanya!*' she called out to Ivan across the cobbles. They had looked at the bullet holes in the church tower, gone through the parsonage and bought a postcard of Emily's dog, Keeper, as they came out at the other end.

'And we saw his collar in a glass case,' she said. Then they walked on to the waterfall and Ivan asked where the water had gone to. Myrtle explained that it dried up in the summer time and said he wore a puzzled look all the way home. He was trying to teach her Russian, she said, but she could never remember what that letter was that looked like a spider.

'He's a real Teutonic knight,' she went on, 'He's given me a piece of Baltic amber with a fly in it.'

I looked at the object she held out and it could have been the plastic handle off a screwdriver.

'How do you know it's real?' I asked.

'He says amber's warm, like the heart of Mother Russia.'

'So is plastic,' I said. 'And so's my toothbrush handle.'

'And that might be a bit of black cotton,' said Otley.

Myrtle carried on preparing her rye bread and cashew nut paté and chose to ignore us.

'Ugh!' she said. 'That American stuffing himself with Big Macs, it's revolting.' She swallowed some capsules and asked me if I wanted one, casting knowing looks in the direction of Bobbin Yard.

'Not if they're what I think they are,' I said, concerned about my husband's molecules. They seemed to be adding fuel to Myrtle; she was smouldering like a peat fire these days. I thought it was time to issue a word of warning.

'What'll you do when Ivan goes back?' I asked casually.

'What about?'

'All that libido and nobody to inflict it on.'

She paced the kitchen as if weighing up the pros and cons then came to a conclusion. She would go with him she said.

'But I shall not see him tonight – he has to meet somebody.'

'Where?' said Otley suddenly alert.

'I don't know, he wouldn't tell me.'

Otley excused himself and rushed upstairs to get his binoculars and consult his spying manual. Myrtle sympathized with me as we did the washing up, putting everything back in the wrong place.

'When's he going back to work?' she wanted to know.

• • • • •

That evening while we were watching the nightly dose of wildlife on the box about beetles that, when they were not copulating, rolled balls of dung willy-nilly across the landscape, Tom came in to say that Hank had gone off again after making a mystery phone call. We said it was his business what he did on his holidays but Otley was determined to get to the bottom of it.

'Did he go in the direction of Skartha?'

'Yes,' said Tom. 'He was meeting someone at the Drovers at half-past nine.' We looked at each other. The Drovers was off the beaten track on the high moors, the sort of place you found yourself at by accident. And Ivan was out as well wasn't he?

'That's another thing,' Tom went on. 'I found this in the café after he'd gone out this morning.' He put a piece of crumpled paper on the table and smoothed it out. It seemed to have some personal details on it; Ivan's age, education, job and interests and a telephone number.

'They're double agents I bet,' said Otley.

'Why would they meet at the Drovers when they're both staying here?' I asked.

'To put you off the scent,' he said. 'It's a red herring.'

They needn't bother, I thought, I'm not on the scent. They'd have to go and get them, the men decided, and Freda and I could go along as decoy ducks so we would have to dress up a bit.

'Like Minnehaha and *The Sound of Music*?' I said eagerly.

'No, like Granny Hawkweed,' he snapped. 'This is serious, the country is in danger.'

'Why would they want to spy on us anyway?' said Freda.

'To find out what we know about them,' Tom said.

'And to find out if we know they know,' said Otley.

I went up to the lumber room and found a charcoal grey costume and a bowler hat which I thought needed brightening up a bit so I put on my red moon-boots and pinned a Union Jack over my T-shirt. I wondered where Mike was and stopped to look through his keyhole on the way downstairs. I couldn't see anything but dirty socks. I would have to write him a letter; then there were footsteps behind.

'I'm here,' Mike said. 'Did you want something?'

'There's chicken and salad in the fridge,' I said. 'I'm off now.'

'Where are you going dressed like that?' he inquired.

'Spying,' I said. 'Don't wait up for us.'

. . . . .

Otley took the wheel. He had not taken his tablets and was in a mean mood; it was as well to go along with him in the circumstances. We flew along the silver road at a good lick, through dark plantations and well-lit council estates, by chattering streams and sullen bogs. After a while I felt I was suffering from jet lag and thought we should be there by now.

'Wasn't that the crossroads?'

'We've passed it three times,' said Freda. 'It's here again.'

'I thought you'd like a run round,' said Otley as he parked on a patch of dirt with wire netting round it that did for a car park.

'You go in first,' he said to me. 'He won't recognize you in that hat.'

I pulled my bowler down over my eyes and marched boldly through to the Ladies; there was no point in sneaking about pretending I wasn't there. I took in the scene from a glass panel in the door then went into the snug and asked for a shandy. There was a young couple eating each other and they paid no attention to me so I was able to examine the public bar at my leisure.

There was a red-faced farmer with one of those bifocal hats on like Sherlock Holmes; a furtive couple in walking gear sneaking a bite of their sandwiches when they thought nobody was looking; two local Vikings on an evening of rape and pillage; and yes, in the corner by the door so he could make a quick getaway, was Hank. He was talking to a young man with hair like a scrubbing-brush and a military bearing. As I watched, Hank took something out of his hip pocket and passed it over the table to his companion. They clasped hands briefly and the younger man put the item into his own pocket. It looked as if Otley was on to something. I left my shandy and hurried back with the news.

'Bastards!' said Otley.

'What are we going to do?' I asked.

'When they come out we'll throw a sack over their heads,' he said, 'and you and Freda tie them up.'

'Shall we put them in the stocks?' I said, getting carried away.

'First sensible thing you've said all day!' said Otley.

I had second thoughts. As my husband was on head tablets, I reasoned, what he thought was right must be wrong. In which case what was I doing here? Should I go home and send for the doctor? But by the time he got there Otley would have calmed down and be sat reading *David Copperfield* and the doctor would say, 'Don't get excited Mrs Craven, it doesn't help to exaggerate.'

It was easier to ride the storm than fight it but I suggested giving them a cup of tea like we did the German paratroops in the war.

'They didn't give our lads cups of tea,' said Otley.

'They weren't dressed as nuns,' I explained.

We settled down to wait and Otley turned his collar up like Humphrey Bogart in *The Maltese Falcon* then produced a water-pistol from the glove compartment. He had come by it accidentally when he was five years old; Granny had sent him to the shop for a packet of Bisto and he came back with a water-pistol instead. It had been used for spraying the aspidistras since he grew up.

Freda handed round some liquorice allsorts and wished she had brought her knitting, she was fed up with us sitting there staring at each other.

'Don't take all the coconut ones,' said Otley as I put my hand into the bag.

'They don't grow liquorice in Pontefract now,' said Freda.

'They can't get anybody to pick it,' said Tom.

'Was that chap Russian-looking?' asked Otley.

'No, more Ashley Wilkes-looking but with a short back and sides.'

'What's he look like then?' he asked.

'Blond, elegant, and with an old-fashioned respect for the fair sex,' I drooled. 'He's in *Gone with the Wind.*'

'I bet the fair sex had an old-fashioned respect for him too,' said Otley, looking to Tom for moral support.

'No Greenham Common women there,' said Tom.

I couldn't let the side down so I said the Greenham Common women have a point, there's no defence against a nuclear holocaust.

'I always thought you were a lesbian,' said Otley.

'Where does this liquorice come from then?' Freda mused.

'Asia Minor,' said Tom.

'I thought it tasted funny,' she said, spitting it out.

• • • • •

Presently the door of the pub opened and the figures of Hank and his accomplice appeared bathed in light as if about to be beamed up in *Star Trek*. We got out of the car as quietly as we could with Freda still clutching the bag of sweets.

'Shh . . .!' Otley hissed like a bad-tempered camel.

When they drew level with us we leapt out of the dark and overpowered them and squashed them into the car on the back seat between Freda and me.

'Don't try any fancy tricks,' Otley said, pushing the pistol into their ribs. 'We've got you covered.'

'Are you guys crazy?' said Hank through the sack. I wanted to say yes but thought better of it. I found some manicure scissors in my handbag and cut a hole in the sacks so they could breathe and Freda pushed a sweet into their mouths.

'No coconut ones left I'm afraid,' she apologized.

'I know that voice, it's Mrs Arncliff isn't it?' said Hank.

'Sorry we had to do this – security,' I told them.

'And that sounds like Mrs Craven.'

'You can talk when we get home,' said Otley. 'And you'd better come clean.'

I stared at the road unwinding like a satin ribbon beneath us; the moon watched us, smirking through the rear window and then sometimes peeped in at the side. What would Kit be doing now, I wondered. Painting his little pictures in his little bachelor den, nobody to tidy his brushes or make him a cup of cocoa. I hardly dared let myself think of him. Wasn't that a bunch of periwinkle sticking out of his back pocket the other day? Where was he going with it? Suddenly the brakes screeched and we came to a halt outside a fish and chip shop.

'Anybody want fish 'n' chips?' said Otley.

'Oo! yes,' we said.

'What about you two?' he said to the sacks. They nodded and shuffled their feet.

'If you'll oblige by untying us,' said Hank.

'And don't try anything funny,' Tom said, freeing them.

'Do you want salt and vinegar?' inquired Otley.

'Just vinegar for me,' said Hank.

'No vinegar on mine,' said his companion. 'No salt either.'

'Make your mind up then,' said Otley.

'Do you like mushy peas?' Freda asked them.

'Try anything once.'

'Six lots of mushy peas then,' Freda ordered, 'and we'll take them home and have them properly with bread and butter.'

'Hallelujah!' said Hank.

We took our captives to the Mill House and sat them down at Freda's white formica table assuring them they would not be harmed if they told us everything they knew.

'What about?' asked Hank.

If they refused to co-operate, Otley warned, we would have to try sensory deprivation. Hank laughed. How did we know the difference?

'I give in,' he said. 'Whaddya wanna know?'

'Who's your contact?' Otley asked him. 'We saw you passing messages; you didn't know you were being watched.'

'This here's ma grandson, Fontaine, lootenant in the United States Army. He's at the missile site on . . .'

'We like to keep it quiet,' the young man broke in. 'We don't want no trouble – these Greenham Common women are everywhere.'

This struck a sympathetic chord in our menfolk and the tension eased visibly. They understood how it was, women should stay in the kitchen where they belong. But the message? They had been seen.

'It's his birthday,' said Hank. 'I slipped him some dollar bills.'

'These guys are on the ball I'll say that,' said Fontaine.

'THAT COMMIE'S the one you want to get after,' Hank told us the next morning. 'Sumpin' fishy about him, they don't let 'em out on their own.'

He seemed a decent enough chap we said, couldn't tell him from anybody else when he'd got his Marks & Spencer jeans on.

'And he's got an honest face,' Freda said later over coffee. 'I'd buy a second-hand Bendix off him any day.'

'You mean a car don't you?' Tom corrected her.

'I don't drive,' said Freda. 'I only know about washing.'

'Anyway, they're just the ones you've got to watch,' said Otley who was convinced the Red Army would come swarming over Ridings Fell any day now and was making his plans. We would invite them to a party, get them drunk, then bash them on the head with the meat-tenderizer and store them in the cellar. He had worked out the statistics and it should hold about seventy-five of them packed in like sardines; when it was full we would seal the door up with Polyfilla.

'There'll be another ten million of them outside,' said Tom.

'Well, every little helps,' Otley told him.

'I don't like violence,' Freda shuddered. 'Couldn't we just put sleeping tablets in their cocoa?'

'They're not having my Mogadon,' said Otley.

'What about putting rat poison in their samwidges?' said Julian.

'Or making their cabbage soup with hemlock?' I suggested.

'Toadstools on toast?' said Julian for another try.

'Ammonia in their vodka?' said Tom.

'The danger with all that,' said Otley wisely, 'is that we might get it first if we're hungry.'

'We don't want any bloodshed,' I told him.

'No,' said Freda, 'not when we've just had the place done up.'

'Leave it to me, I know how to fell them,' Otley assured us. 'Like bullocks in a slaughter house.'

The door slammed which meant that Mike was home; we wanted his opinion but he refused to have anything to do with his father's schemes. He was upstairs and behind locked doors before you could say Burgess and Maclean and I felt I was becoming alienated from this young man who had once been our little angel. What had become of the good Samaritan who turned up with five snotty-nosed little varmints from Monkey Park and asked,

'Mam, can I have six bananas?'

Now he wrote rude things on lavatory walls and Otley promised to give him an earful but never did. I would have to write him a letter.

'Dear Boy,' it would say,

> If I am correctly informed, your recent behaviour leaves much to be desired. It is not the way of a gentleman to chalk 'Theophilus Umpleby is a faggot' on the walls of the Public Convenience. Mr Umpleby is a member of the Low Riding Swedenborgian Church and has been with the Bradford & Bingley for twenty-five years.
>
> I much enjoyed your account of the workings of your GT521 LW/MW/VHF DIGITAL CLOCK RADIO/ALARM WITH LIGHT and anxiously await the answers to the many questions I have asked you. Adieu.

In the films Daddy always sorted it out with folksy parables while Mummy cried into her best lace handkerchief. I wandered out into the garden to pick some roses and found myself thinking of Kit and a little thatched cottage with roses round the door like on the calendars. The children romped round him as he painted a Madonna and Child for the village church and he could control them with a look, a word: 'Leave your mother alone, she's tired,' he would say, and we would all go gathering firewood together.

The dream was shattered as Stalin went by with his malodorous bucket, corduroys whistling like a linnet.

'Nah then,' he called.

'How's George?' I asked.

'He don't trust me, he's gone back to his mother,' he said, dropping his bucket with a clang on the cobbles.

'He knows you're going to eat him,' I said.

I was with Myrtle on this. Easter brought smiling farmers with curly little lambkins in their arms. Everybody said Ah! and then went home to their lamb chops and green peas.

'Aye,' said Stalin. 'He'd be right tasty wi' a bit o' apple sauce.'

This cheered me up no end as I realized how lucky I was not to be in George's shoes, or trotters.

'Have you gone mad?' asked Otley when he caught me singing in the kitchen.

. . . . .

That evening we went over to Freda's to look at her portrait in the style of a Dutch interior: sitting at her formica table smiling at a bowl of apples, a merry baby on the floor playing with a dead pheasant.

'She's only got one eye,' said Julian.

'And one leg,' said Tom, scrutinizing if from all angles. 'I can only see one clog.'

'If you're going to nitpick,' said Kit, 'I'll paint somebody else in future; there's such a thing as artistic licence.'

'What's that?' asked Julian.

'It means you can paint what you like.'

'Well what was I doing sitting there like a wet lettuce?' Freda said. 'You can paint what you like at home.'

We had just settled down to enjoy a quiet drink when Tom fished a piece of paper out of his pocket and held it out.

'It's another one,' he said, passing it to Otley first. 'He threw it in the litter bin and I picked it out straight away.'

'Good man!' said Otley.

The letter, addressed to Ivan, was written on violet-scented paper in a bold, round hand. 'Meet me at the Trocadero Tea Dance in Quarry Bottoms at five o'clock on Wednesday,' it said. 'I shall be wearing a pink carnation.'

'Why can't they wear dandelions?' asked Julian. 'It's always carnations.'

'Shut up!' said Tom.

'We shall have to shadow them,' said Otley.

'Don't tell Myrtle, she'll know soon enough,' I warned.

'It's a long time since we went to the Trocadero,' said Freda. 'I don't know what to put on.'

'Wear that blue frock again, I liked you in that,' Tom told her, much to her annoyance as she had torn it up for dusters long ago.

'Wear that red one, like Captain Scarlet,' said Julian.

'And don't bring any liquorice allsorts,' added Otley.

We searched the building for any sign of bugging but we were not sure what we were looking for. Had they got wires attached? Were they disguised as plastic daffodils? or did they go in holes in the wall like rawlplugs? Otley said they can take pictures through your keyhole with optical fibres, wear plastic nipples with radio transmitters in them and even swallow silicon chips. He had read all about it in his *Do It Yourself Spy Kit.*

It was late when Myrtle came in from learning Russian on the moors with Ivan, goose-grass in her hair and sticking to her body-warmer. She flopped into an armchair with a deep sigh.

'He loves Tamari,' she announced suddenly.

'Who's she?' I asked.

'It's sauce made out of soya beans,' she said reverently, and I had to say it had never come my way.

'Where did you eat?' I said for a talking point.

'The Chinese takeaway in Quarry Bottoms. We had chop suey, mushy peas and chips – I took the meat out of it first though.'

'Did you enjoy it?' I asked.

'No,' she said and I made a mental note never to go there.

Myrtle had gone all ethnic with buckwheat pancakes and bortsch, and sour cream with her strawberries instead of

Wall's ice cream like we usually had. It was a healthier life-style than ours she said.

'It is if you don't get caught,' said Otley.

'We're going on the Trans-Siberian Railway to Vladivostock,' she said nonchalantly, examining her finger-nails.

'What for?' I inquired.

'He says Siberia's lovely in the spring time,' she said, taking a handful of libido pills.

'Anyway,' I said. 'It'll be a change from Blackpool.'

'Keep away from those salt mines,' Otley warned her.

'It's not all salt mines,' Myrtle said indignantly.

'It is if you're down 'em,' said Otley.

He wanted to know what they talked about. Did Ivan question her about anything in particular? Where did he learn English? Why was he teaching her Russian? Did his nipples feel normal? Myrtle refused to answer any more questions after the last one.

'Is he having one of his funny turns again?' she whispered to me behind his back.

'He's worried about you,' I lied.

'Don't worry,' she told him. 'If I don't like it I shan't go there again.'

'You can't go there on an Awayday you know,' he said. 'You might not be able to get back.'

'How much is it going to rush you?' I asked.

'I've got enough,' said Myrtle. 'I can draw my Post Office savings out.'

'If you clobber one of the guards in Red Square you'll get there for nothing,' said Otley helpfully.

We said good night and left Myrtle picking the goose-grass out of her hair. Otley seemed elated now that he had got something to work on and I had been advised many times to share his interests. 'Show him that you care,' Miss Armitage always said. 'Pretend you are interested even if you are not,' said Dr Moss. 'It's a small thing to ask.' I racked my brains for something I could say to send him to bed happy; it wasn't easy but I had to say something encouraging.

'You know those seventy-five Russians in the cellar?' I asked him.

'Yes,' he said, his eyes flashing with the light of battle.

'Well if they're skinny you can squash a few more in.'

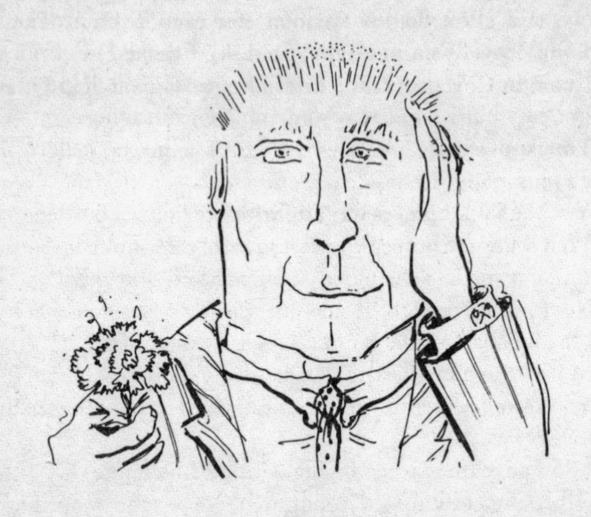

OTLEY SLEPT late the next day. He was so worn out with people mispronouncing words on the box that he couldn't bring himself to get up. I took him some tea and scrambled eggs and opened the window to let the morning sun hit him full in the face. He looked haggard, as if he had run a four-minute mile. I poured out some tea.

'You're not a bad old stick,' he said.

I thought it was a good time to ask him about joining the Ancient Britons' Social Club; they had jolly evenings in the Temperance Hall and Miss Armitage would approve.

'I'm not that far gone!' he spluttered.

'They have a good time,' I said, smoothing his pillow.

'What – a lot of old fogies grumbling about their gas bills.'

'They have sing-songs and all that.'

'"Nelly Dean", crying in their beer, stupid sods!'

'No, that's the British Legion,' I reminded him. 'They have some lovely outings, they go all over the place.'

'I've seen Coventry Cathedral – I'm not going again,' he said.

'They visit stately homes as well . . .' I began.

'I'm not going to Sandringham with a coach load of old nanny-goats wittering on about their arthritis.'

'They went to Morecambe last year,' I told him.

'And got stuck in the bloody quicksands didn't they?'

'Not for long though,' I said cheerfully. 'The tide came in and the lifeboat got them out before they drowned.'

'More's the pity,' he said. 'Is there any more toast?'

'You're a nasty little man aren't you?' I couldn't help saying.

'I don't ask them to go spying with me,' he said.

I started to tidy up the room; there were road maps and field-glasses, wall-charts about the armed services, books about the CIA and the KGB, emergency rations and a survival manual, a Swiss army knife bristling like a metal hedgehog, plastic bags and kitchen foil to keep us warm in the event of a nuclear winter.

'This isn't healthy, you should get out more,' I told him.

'It's too late for me to worry about being healthy,' he said.

I noticed that the floorboards were raised in the corner of the room and his box open with the brass key still in it. It had a blue tag tied on it. Now I knew which key it was I promised myself that one day, when he was out, I would find out the secret once and for all. It was high time Mike knew the answer to his question 'What did you do in the war, Daddy?'

'Don't wear that Union Jack today,' Otley said suddenly. 'We don't want to attract attention.'

It was D-Day for Operation Ivan the Terrible and spying at the Trocadero Tea Dance called for something genteel.

Crooking one's little finger in a bowler hat and red moon-boots wouldn't seem right.

'What do you think I should wear then?' I asked foolishly.

'That flowered one with the red poppies on, in case there's any blood.'

I walked over to the window and looked out over the roof-tops, like Merle Oberon in *The Private Life of Henry VIII* just before she was executed. Would we get out of this alive?

'Isn't it a beautiful day?' I said.

. . . . .

Julian came over to look in our atlas for Nijni Novgorod since it wasn't in his, but it wasn't in ours either, much to his disgust.

'That Ivan's a big liar,' he said. 'He told us his dad was born there.' I thought we should not attach too much importance to this as my dad was born in Boggle Brow and that's not in the atlas either.

'You're not a secret agent are you?' snapped Otley. That's true, I thought, but I might just as well be.

'Keep your eyes peeled when you get back,' Otley told Julian. 'And keep your powder dry.'

'What's he mean?' Julian whispered when Otley's back was turned.

'I don't know,' I whispered back. 'He's been reading *Last of the Mohicans* or something.'

'When we've trapped him I'll see Miss Fidget gets to hear about the part you played,' Otley went on approvingly.

'Oh her!' said Julian. 'Who cares what she thinks?'

We would have to be at the Trocadero first so that it would not look as if we were trailing Ivan. It was a good job Myrtle was out. Ivan said he had to attend a conference in Harrogate so she had gone to join the Friends of the Death-watch Beetle who bought up old churches for the purpose of not restoring them.

'And that's another thing,' said Otley. 'They don't have conferences in Harrogate, they're supposed to stay in London.'

Through the window the village looked so normal. Everybody going about their business of scratching a living. How deceptive appearances can be.

'Don't worry,' said Dr Moss over the phone. 'He's not dangerous; I'll give him some different tablets.'

Freda looked good enough to eat in a strawberry-pink dress, vanilla shoes and handbag, and earrings that looked like white gob-stoppers. She was clutching a bag of sweets.

'I told you not to bring liquorice allsorts,' Otley spat at her.

'They're Fox's glacier mints,' she said. 'I thought they'd be cooler on a hot day like this.'

He snatched them out of her hands and flung them angrily into the road and we scrambled after them like ragamuffins diving for pennies. It was some time before we found them all.

'There's one short,' Freda kept saying.

When we eventually got into the car Otley set off down the road like a bashi-bazouk. The tea dance had started when we got there and the band were scraping away at a selection from *The Gypsy Baron*. Behind them a green, shot silk curtain picked up an eerie light and made them look as if they were in a fish tank. In their dusty beetle suits the ancient musicians looked as if they had been there for ever, like fossilized crustaceans in a rock.

'Bloody hell!' Tom said looking round.

The little tables were all covered with white damask tablecloths of the type you get at funerals, with dark red tablelamps to hide the stains. We put ourselves away in a corner and ordered toasted teacakes and Kunzel cakes.

'I don't think you can get them now,' Freda said. 'They've not had any in Hagenbach's for donkey's years.'

'I don't care,' said Otley.

Suddenly for no reason the music changed to a medley of Beatles numbers and everybody stamped their feet in time to 'We All Live in a Yellow Submarine'. Otley's lips clamped into a bloodless line.

'I can't stand it,' he said. 'That and *Pink Panther* music.'

'Teacakes are nice aren't they?' Freda inquired.

'Too many currants in,' said Otley.

'I thought it was sultanas you didn't like,' observed Freda.

'I don't like currants either,' said Otley as he decorated the edge of his plate with them. 'But not as much as I don't like sultanas.'

There were seven gaudily iced cakes on a thick plate with a paper doyley and Tom considered this outrageous.

'It's not even two apiece,' he gasped.

'We'll ask for another,' I suggested.

'We don't want to bother the waitress, she's run off her feet,' said Freda. 'I know, I've had a packet.'

'You have two each and I'll have the coffee one,' I said in a spirit of self-sacrifice.

'We can't let you do that, it's not fair!' protested Freda.

'It's a good cup of tea,' Tom commented.

'I know,' said Freda, picking up a knife ready to operate on the cakes. 'We'll eat the four pink ones, let the boys have a chocolate one each and you and me can share the coffee one.'

'We're supposed to be spying,' Otley scolded.

Just then an olive-skinned beauty sat down at the table

nearest the cloakroom and we were stunned into silence. Wearing an apricot velvet two-piece with a carnation tucked into her bosom, she had just the right exotic allure for a Mata Hari.

'Don't all look at once,' said Otley as we scrutinized her.

I slipped out to the cloakroom to make sure the windows were locked and had a good look at her as I went past. She would not be able to give us the slip I assured my husband and, yes, that was lemon tea she was drinking. That was the good news, now for the bad – that was not a pink carnation she was wearing.

'It's not?'

'No, it's a white one with pink edges.'

We wrestled with this problem for a while until Freda came up with the answer.

'Perhaps they'd sold out of pink ones.'

I was just adding hot water to the pot and stirring up the anaemic result when Ivan walked in with a pretty blonde; a sort of northern Grace Kelly, cool but with a blunt edge. In a blue shirtwaister with a pink carnation tucked into the belt – she had to be the one. Freda hurriedly took a chair from the next table and Tom found another one so we squashed ourselves up to make room for them.

'What a lovely surprise seeing you here,' I lied.

'Who's the fair lady?' inquired Otley in a tone of voice I had never heard him use before.

'Dyoryeen Dyiggulye,' said Ivan tying his tongue in a knot.

'From Halifax,' she said, helping him out.

She had a gift shop in the Piece Hall and sold Welsh dolls, Irish linen tea-towels, woolly sheep from Scotland, silk diaries from Shanghai, wind chimes from Taiwan and bamboo pencils with tassels on from Hong Kong.

'All foreign stuff is it?' Otley asked casually. 'Haven't you got anything English?'

Doreen thought hard for a minute or two then remembered there were some stickers in a drawer saying 'Maggie Out' and 'Europe Get Stuffed'.

The sweating fiddlers mopped their brows while the pianist filled in with a boogie and the frantic dancers fell over each other in their anxiety to abandon the floor.

'How did you two come to meet then?' asked Otley.

Ivan looked at Doreen and moved his head slightly.

'That's our secret,' she said.

'Have you got something to hide then?' Tom asked bluntly.

'I'll say we have,' said Doreen with a wink.

Freda dropped her handkerchief and we both bent down to pick it up, crashing our heads together under the table.

'She's clever,' I said. 'Tell the truth and nobody believes you.'

'And bold as brass,' she said, blowing up my nose like Barbara Woodhouse. We surfaced together and Ivan looked bemused. The band, fighting fit again, went into a tango and a swarthy little man with patent leather hair took the floor, ducking and weaving like a prize-fighter, until his old knees gave way under the strain of supporting his fat friend in a dip that got out of hand. She sank to the ground, corsets creaking, and lay like a stranded whale.

'Do you tango?' I asked Ivan.

'Yis fascyist,' he said, shaking his head.

'Oh! We dance proletarian as well,' I assured him. '"Knees Up Mother Brown" and all that stuff.'

The band played a selection from *The Desert Song* and then 'Red Sails in the Sunset' to sign off with so Otley had to move quickly. He leaned confidentially towards Doreen.

'What's a nice girl like you doing mixed up in this?' he asked.

'It's exciting,' she said. 'Adds a bit of spice to life.'

'You'll get more than you bargained for,' he cautioned.

'It's not the first time I've done it,' she said cryptically, 'and it won't be the last.'

'Who's your contact?' asked Otley, fingering the cake knife menacingly.

'I met him through the bureau.'

'Aha!'

Suddenly everybody moved towards the cloakroom like a shoal of herring. It was time to go.

'Come back with us for a drink,' I had been instructed to say. 'We can run you over to Halifax in the morning.'

'Ooh! Thanks, that'll be smashing.'

We all squashed into the car and Freda handed round the Fox's glacier mints. I noticed Otley take the water-pistol out of the glove compartment and put it in his pocket.

'Isn't it a lovely day?' I said, looking out of the window.

WE SAT our guests down under the fluorescent light in Freda's white fitted kitchen and I suggested wearing sunglasses in case we got snow-blindness.

'It wouldn't be the third degree then,' Otley said crossly. He paced the room with his shoulder to one side like Colombo, then stopped and swirled round suddenly.

'Nijni Novgorod,' he said accusingly.

'I beg your pardon,' said Doreen.

'Where is Nijni Novgorod?' he repeated slowly.

'Blowed if I know – isn't it near Timbuktu?' she said. Otley turned impatiently to Ivan.

'Your father was born there,' he mouthed.

'*Da*,' said Ivan.

Otley produced an atlas and opened it at the page headed 'Union of Soviet Socialist Republics'. He laid it on the table in front of Ivan and shouted into his ear.

'Is not here.'

'*Niet*,' said Ivan.

'Then where is it?'

'Yis Gorky now.'

We remembered then that the name had been changed but Otley was not one to give up so easily. He turned to Doreen:

'The game's up, comrades; you will not be allowed to leave until you name your accomplices.'

'He can't do that,' she explained. 'He's got to give them time to get away.'

'So you admit it?' he pounced.

'It's not your business anyway,' she said, 'who I associate with. My Auntie Alice knows and she's very particular.'

'Soviet citizens are not at liberty to wander about on their own willy-nilly,' Otley persisted.

'Wiollyi-niollyi?' said Ivan, mystified.

'Have a sandwich,' Freda said, passing round a plate.

'It's nice potted meat,' said Doreen. 'Is it from Sainsbury's?'

'Our butcher – he's the parish councillor,' we told her.

'Oh!' she said.

'I put it to you,' Otley went on, 'that your interest is in the missile base at Skartha.'

'*Niet*,' said Ivan, helping himself to another sandwich.

'You were seen taking photographs of the CND sign on Giant Rombald's backside,' Otley said, playing his trump card.

'*Niet*,' said Ivan.

'Are you or are you not going on the march with Myrtle?'

'Who's Myrtle?' asked Doreen.

'Our cousin,' we told her. 'She lives here.'

'You realize I shall have to call in the police,' Otley said.

'My Auntie Alice'll wonder where I've got to,' Doreen sobbed. 'I said I'd get her surgical stocking and elastic bandages.'

'Don't give me that sob-stuff,' Otley sneered. 'This isn't Jackanory.'

'*Niet*,' said Ivan.

'Why did you do it?' asked Otley leaning over the table and looking into her eyes. 'A nice girl like you a traitor!'

'I contacted the bureau,' she sniffed, 'and they put me in touch with Ivan.'

'Which bureau?'

'Did you say traitor?' asked Doreen, suddenly alert.

'The name of the bureau please,' demanded Otley sternly.

'It's the Find a Mate Computadate – I saw it in the Sunday papers; it's only fifty pounds and nothing more to pay until you're satisfied.' Doreen and Ivan gave each other a smouldering look. They were both clearly satisfied.

'*Da!*' he said, 'I marryi you.'

He had jumped ship in Ullapool, she said, and they thought if they married he might be allowed to stay here but it would mean lying low for a while.

'All this fuss,' Freda said. 'I could have been getting on with my knitting.'

'You can't be too careful these days,' said Tom. 'Is there any of that treacle pudding left from dinner-time?'

'No,' said Freda.

'Well I hope you're going to apologize for putting these nice young people to all this trouble,' I said to Otley.

'I was only joking,' he said, squirting them with his water-pistol. 'This isn't a real gun.'

It was too late by then to run Doreen back to Halifax so we poured out some drinks and had some bacon-flavoured crisps.

'Fancy waking up in the night and finding that lot staring at you,' she said when I put her in the museum room. I gave the stuffed creatures a quick dust and assured her they were all dead.

We heard the door slam and the floorboards creak on the landing. Doreen was afraid it was a ghost.

'It's only my son,' I told her. 'He's just been out for a while. He tells me everything.'

IVAN LEFT Myrtle a note saying he had to attend a conference in Gretna Green and would she like to finish up his stir-fry vegetables. She went quiet for a day or two and sat up in the attic listening to 'For All We Know We May Never Meet Again' and then went to the CND meeting in an emerald-green frock with purple spots.

'Bloody foreigners!' she said.

Otley seemed to take it well every time Nancy went off with Hank Waldorf. It wasn't like him.

'Wait till he goes home,' he said. 'She'll want me back.'

'You won't have her back will you?' asked Freda.

'Yes I will,' he said.

He had always wanted to be a Muslim with four wives, he said. One was no good to man or beast. It was natural, like the bees flitting from flower to flower. He'd been like that ever since he saw Yul Brynner in *The King and I*.

'You'll get AIDS,' we warned him.

If you're a secret agent, it appeared, you needed a woman in every port like the sailors. In which case, I thought, he won't mind if I have one extra now and again. Would he mind if I popped over to Kit's this evening while he was watching *World in Action*.

'You're disarranging my molecules again,' he said. 'I've only just got them settled from last time.'

I was beginning to regard him as one of those Mickey Mouse faces with holes that you have to shake little silver balls into.

'Sorry,' I lied.

The museum was turning out to be what is known in the world of finance as a loss-maker. The only visitors were a few locals who were curious to know if we still had the same wallpaper with the jam tarts on in Granny Hawkweed's bedroom, and a little boy who was fascinated by a picture of the Diamond Jubilee and wondered if Queen Victoria was a tea-cosy. At this rate of fifty pences we could expect to earn seven pounds a week in the high season.

'Let's all go to Torremolinos,' said Freda, looking for her holiday brochure.

'I'm not going there,' said Otley. 'To be separated by the Basque Separatists!'

He'd already told us he was going shark fishing hadn't he and somebody saw three Japanese in Haworth the other day. He'd have to keep his eyes open – coming all that way, making out they wanted to see where Heathcliff lived.

And Mike was doing his turn at The Flying Shuttle this week, I reminded him; it was only right we should give him moral support. Dr Moss wanted him to take part in normal family life as a counter-balance to his involvement in international affairs.

'You don't call that normal what he does,' he jeered.

The afternoon sun shone on the pretty bubbles in the washing-up water and turned them into little rainbows. How charming! I thought as they ran off my elbows and down the front of my apron.

'Is my blue shirt clean?' inquired my husband.

It was clean, I assured him, but it was waiting to be ironed. Well the fairies wouldn't do it, he informed me. I tried to negotiate a deal. If he would finish the washing-up I would iron his shirt.

'Washing-up is woman's work,' he said.

'You'll have to do it when I'm dead,' I told him.

He picked up the oven-gloves to strangle me with but Mike came in and he put them down.

'I can't make out whether you're a lesbian or you've joined the Militant Tendency,' he said.

'Can I borrow your wig for a laff?' asked Mike.

'Of course, I'll go and get it for you,' I said pleasantly.

'If you tell me where it is I'll get it myself,' he said.

'The door's locked,' I said feeling guilty.

'Why do you lock your door?' asked Mike in amazement.

'For the same reason that you do,' I said nastily.

'She wants to be a person,' said Otley sniggering.

. . . . .

I sneaked over to Bobbin Yard in the evening to see if the poor lonely man wanted any shopping doing and he gave me a pile of socks to mend. I tried not to sit too close but it wasn't easy. He went mad the other night, he explained, when he saw me in that Indian get-up; *Hiawatha* had always been his favourite poem.

'It must have been the feathers,' I sympathized.

We looked at a coffee-table book on the Old Masters but

there seemed to be a lot of naked women lying about like big fat slugs. It wasn't necessary, I couldn't help thinking.

'You're not happy with him,' Kit said eventually. 'I know you love me.' I didn't know how to tell him that I loved him but hated his beard; artists were such delicate, sensitive creatures.

'He's sick,' I said loyally.

'Come away with me,' he urged. I could never desert my husband and family, I told him gently, it just wouldn't be right.

'I don't mean for good,' he said. 'Only for the weekend.'

'Not even for the weekend,' I had to say, realizing for the first time that I had a yellow streak. There was a brass band in Jubilee Park on Sunday afternoon he said, but brass bands give me migraine. A Civil War weekend at East Riddlesden Hall with skirmishing on the lawns perhaps? Oh no! Last time a cannon-ball ran amok and frightened the horses.

'We can have a Dales Wayfarer to Pateley Bridge,' he said, pouring out some plonk, 'and come back by Brimham Rocks.'

'I've been,' I said. I was getting like my husband.

'We can go on a Midweek Boomerang to London,' he said, 'and feed the ducks in St James's Park.'

'We've got some ducks here,' I reminded him. 'On the Leeds and Liverpool Canal.

'I thought you loved me.'

'I do, I do.'

'Well then?'

'Just because I love you it doesn't mean I don't love my husband,' I explained.

'Don't trifle with my affections,' he said sadly, making me feel like a cad. I gave his hand a quick squeeze and we kissed. It was like falling into a blackberry bush but nice with it. We looked at more paintings and listened to some *Mastermind* music on Radio Three and then it was time to go.

'Mike's doing a turn at the pub on Saturday,' I told him. 'It's going to be sensational; will you be there?'

'No,' he said.

• • • • •

The Man in the Moon was watching as I ran across the cobbles, I don't know what he thought about all the goings on down here. Somebody brushed past me in the shadows. It looked like a Japanese. I must remember to tell Otley.

'Where have you been to?' he said when I got in.

'Out,' I said, drawing the curtains. 'That was a Japanese I just ran into, I think.'

'You're mad!' he said. 'It was old Inky Popplewell coming back from their Audrey's.'

I made cocoa and sandwiches as Tom and Freda had come over for a game of Scrabble. Otley won every time because he altered the rules when it was his turn, and kept looking in the dictionary when it was our turn and saying it wasn't in. Then he switched the box on and we were just in time to see ten thousand flying bogongs copulating upside down, only to be roasted by the Aborigines and eaten like salted peanuts. Then there was a grey suede caterpillar called Hercules having a struggle undressing himself, and a brown-and-orange caterpillar carrying flick-knives.

'It is not possible to sex a caterpillar,' said the disappointed narrator, turning to elephants.

'They're sex-maniacs,' said Freda. 'There was a programme on about the sex life of flowers the other day.'

'We saw it,' I told her.

'They poke their filthy noses into everything,' she went on.

'It makes the world go round,' said Tom, giving Otley a wink.

'You speak for yourself,' she said.

THE CABARET was Mike's idea. He said we would have to do something to liven the place up if we were going to attract an international clientele. Sophisticated jet-setters would expect more than Bath buns and a selection from *Call me Madam*.

Otley dressed with great care in a green silk shirt that brought out the hard glinting green of his eyes.

'You look nice,' I said, because Miss Armitage said I had to let him know he was loved.

'I know,' he said. 'Can you lend me a tenner?'

Myrtle wore a cream linen suit with a gold kid belt, her new-penny hair in corkscrew crinkles. I loosened the belt on my barn-dancing skirt and decided to go back on a diet. We found our favourite backs-to-the-wall position in the pub, in case we were attacked, and sat opposite a picture of Karl Marx.

'They've got him outside, what do they want him in here for?' Otley complained looking the other way.

'Port and lemon for the ladies,' Tom called.

'Not for me,' I said. 'Port gives me a headache.'

'What'll you have then?'

'Shandy please.'

'You can't get drunk on shandy,' Tom said.

'She's a right misery-guts,' Otley told everybody.

Hank leaned over the bar afraid to stand upright in case he brained himself on the oak beams. He was talking earnestly to Nancy whose earrings jangled as she pulled the pints.

'Poor thing!' said Myrtle. 'He'll be telling her about his boll-weevils.'

The old inn had been built in the days of Samuel Pepys when spitting-sheets were all the rage, and warning notices were everywhere. 'Mind the step', 'Uneven flagstones', 'This is not an exit', and 'Beware of the Dog'. Wolf, the Alsatian, lurked outside tethered to an iron ring, and gnashed his teeth at one and all, tangling himself up in his chain in an effort to get at the customers.

'Nice doggy,' said the nervous, backing away from him.

The whitewashed walls were festooned with pictures of oblong rams and chapel outings to Bridlington and Southport. The prize exhibit was a pair of Cromwell's boots in a glass case, though nobody was sure how they got there. Pewter tankards hung from the low beams; you would have to be very thirsty to want to drink out of them.

'It's a wonder they didn't get lead poisoning,' said Freda.

'Your round,' said Tom.

'A Snowball for me please,' Freda ordered.

'Shandy again for me,' I said.

'You don't want shandy every time,' said Tom. 'Let your

hair down.' I hesitated, thinking I would rather have a cup of tea.

'Make your mind up then,' said Otley, waving my money about.

'What's your favourite tipple?' asked Tom sociably.

'I don't like to say – it's so expensive,' I told him.

'Well, what is it?' he insisted.

'Green Chartreuse,' I said.

'Bloody Hell,' said Tom.

'If you have that you can't have anything else,' Otley warned me.

'I'll have a shandy then,' I said.

Presently the lights dimmed and the landlord blew into the microphone making a nasty, crackling noise, like the scrunching of a thousand packets of potato crisps.

'Ladies and Gentlemen,' he announced, 'it is my pleasure to present to you our very own talented trio "Steam". Give 'em a big hand folks!'

Loudspeakers exploded into life as three exotic creatures came into view. A young lady with spikes on her head sang something incomprehensible. Wearing a red skirt and green Dick Whittington boots, white Garibaldi blouse and a black lace shawl, she banged herself on the head now and again with a tambourine.

'Isn't that Susan Mitchell?' asked Freda, dipping a finger in her Snowball. 'Mother was in the Girls' Life Brigade and cried every time she had to put that pancake hat on.'

'Mike said she was joining the group,' I lied.

'I can't hear what she's singing about,' said Tom.

Mike leapt about like Rudolf Nureyev in *The Corsair*, a red rag round his forehead and my baggy jogging pants on. When he stopped his knee kept on moving.

'Has he got a bad leg?' inquired Myrtle.

'Not that we know of,' said Otley unconcerned.

'I should get it X-rayed if I were you,' she said. 'It keeps giving way.'

'He wouldn't go,' I said.

Now he jumped up and down like an ape and the girls went wild, waving mop-heads made out of purple ostrich feathers. Then he came over to our table and snarled at us before making way for Dirk.

'That's my son,' I told the next table. 'He's not always like that.' I thought I heard them say 'I should hope not', but I couldn't be sure.

Dirk played the keyboard in pink ballet tights, Grandad shirt, mackintosh and sunglasses, his thin blond hair trailing in tendrils like a killer jelly fish.

He bit his bottom lip and nodded in all directions, performed with his right hand, kicking out with his left leg, and then abandoned the keyboard in favour of hopping sideways on his left leg and stamping with his right foot at the same time.

'I don't know how they do that,' said Tom. 'It's harder than patting your head and rubbing your belly.'

The girls screamed as he ran panting back to the keyboard to sing 'Imagine' with Susan pretending to be Yoko Ono. Then we all sang 'Yellow Submarine' and stamped our feet.

'I'm off,' said Otley. 'I can't stand this!'

Fat Mr and Mrs Butterfield sang a selection from *Oliver* but it was hard going trying to see him as the Artful Dodger.

'It's all right with your eyes shut,' Freda said.

The village headman joined us, squeezing in beside Myrtle. She edged away from him, grimacing.

'Don't mind me asking but have you had a bath since you came out of that charnel house?'

'I've done better than that, I've sold out to old Stalin.'

'What for?' we wanted to know. It seemed he had always fancied Myrtle but his butcher's shop had come between them, now there was no excuse. And no muckin' abaht! Would she or wouldn't she? She was worth ten of that Nancy, showing her tits.

'She's a well-made lass, she can't help it,' said Tom.

'She should strap 'em down then like them geisha gels. I see enough tripe in my line of business.'

Mrs Butterfield sat down to eat a pork pie while Mr Butterfield sang 'You Gotta Picka Pocket or Two' with his gold watch chain jangling on his waistcoat buttons. Was that a Japanese sneaking out the back way behind the curtains? I must go and find Otley. He was sitting in the car park under Karl Marx, shoulders bowed in dejection.

'They're trying to destroy me,' he said.

'How do you mean?'

'"Yellow Submarine" in there and *Pink Panther* on the bloody telly at home – I can't stand it.'

'Never mind,' I coaxed. 'Let's have another drink.'

'I hope you're not going to ask for Green Chartreuse,' he said.

'I'll have a shandy,' I promised.

'All right then.'

The landlord blew into the microphone and made a noise like a monsoon followed by a banshee wail.

'Ladies and Gentlemen,' he said. 'There's something in the air, two happy couples announce their engagement – Myrtle Hawkweed and our leading citizen Billy Delph. Give 'em a cheer. And your own little barperson Nancy Blinks is to become the bride of our American buddy Hank Waldorf. Let's hear it for love!'

Otley looked bereft but I pretended not to notice and

joined in the 'Knees Up Mother Brown' stampede. When we were too drunk to stand up they turned us out and we staggered home, tripping on the cobbles. Wolf got somebody by the ankle and we had to send frantically for the ambulance. Poor Otley, what could I say to cheer him up?

'You know those seventy-five Russians in the cellar?' I asked him.

'Shut up!' he said.

WE SAW Hank off with a gift of produce from the allotment.

'Gee thanks!' he said. 'Real Yorkshire rhubarb.'

'Well, we don't grow liquorice any more,' said Freda.

A tear rolled down Nancy's cheek as big as the diamond solitaire on her finger as she clung lovingly to his coat lapels.

'It's his wallet she's crying for,' said Otley who was suffering from sour grapes. He was fed up and going to Cornwall soon. He would leave his room unlocked so that I could clean it out. No he didn't want me to go with him, he wanted to get away from me – give his molecules a rest.

'I haven't done anything,' I said.

'What with you and Miss Armitage.'

In the meantime he had to have a word with the gypsies about Tansy not going to school and we could have a look for those fly Japanese while we were up on the moors.

It was one of those cool, green days that make the red geraniums seem redder. A blue plastic laundry bag hung in the hedge among the wild roses and a half-eaten currant bun came floating down the beck. It would be like this on the moon in a hundred years' time.

We passed the Ancient Britons eating their sandwiches with a belligerent ram standing in front of them.

'Don't look at him and he'll go away,' their leader was saying.

The aroma of rabbit stew grew stronger as we neared Bilberry Cottage and Zelda came out to bid us cross her palm with silver. Her dark hair, once bleached, ran in three colours down her back. Black at the top, red in the middle and yellow at the tips – like the Celtic hero Cuchulain.

Our fortunes were roughly the same. We had come through a hard time but things would be better from now on. Somebody close to us was not to be trusted, we would get a letter from overseas and we would meet a tall, dark, handsome stranger.

'What, all of us?' said Otley.

It seemed that Tansy would not go to school because the other kids called her a gyppo and Rowan was going to report them to the Race Relations Board.

'Well she is gyppo, isn't she?' said Tom.

'If Prince Charles can put up with being called a Pommie Bastard,' said Otley, 'I'm sure you can stand being called gyppos.'

'And if you report it,' I said, 'they'll be after you for your income tax.'

Rowan was making fur gloves out of rabbit skins and sharpening his razor at the time, so we thought we'd better order some.

'These are nice,' said Freda. 'How much are they?'

'Five pound to you,' said Rowan.

'That'll be one pound fifty off for income tax so here's three pound fifty,' said Tom, holding out some coins.

'I've bin thinkin',' said Rowan. 'I don't want them nosey parkers comin' round here. I'll forget it this time.'

Tansy came in with a ferret round her neck and Otley gave her some fatherly advice.

'They called me a tyke when I was down in London,' he said.

'What's a tyke?' she asked with the ferret sitting on her head.

'It's a nasty little dog,' I told her.

'And if you don't go to school tomorrow I'll skin yer alive, yer little divil,' said Rowan, brandishing his cut-throat.

'You'll never get a council house carrying on like that,' I said.

'And if you come across any Nips up here don't forget to report it,' Otley cautioned.

'What's a Nip?' asked Tansy while the ferret nibbled her ears.

'They're like tykes and gyppos,' said Otley, 'only yellow.'

. . . . .

'Did you see those two chaps in Fitchet fields?' Freda asked later that evening. 'Dressed all in black, looking at Mussolini and one was wearing dark glasses.'

'Don't say we've got the Mafia here now,' said Otley. Would I go and get him *The Sicilians* from the library?

'It's the tall, dark, handsome strangers,' I pointed out.

'No,' she said. 'One of them was little and fat.'

What were they doing he wanted to know. Nothing, it seemed. It wasn't much to go on but he had better put his holiday off just in case; and we would have to approach it from a different angle. No parties and no bonhomie. Straightforward threats and strong-arm stuff right from the start – that was what they understood.

'You and Freda dress like simple peasants with gnarled hands,' he told us. 'And Myrtle can dress like a whore.'

'I beg your pardon!' said Myrtle.

'Well they want women like that for their gambling dens,' he said. 'We don't want 'em to think there's nobody like that in Low Riding.'

'You'll have to change your Mini for a black Sedan,' Tom said.

'I'm not drawing my money out for that,' Otley told him sharply.

We had to stock up with spaghetti and olive oil and put a table outside with a striped umbrella. Kit could paint us sitting at it chatting animatedly while we watched their comings and goings.

'I hope they don't bring the Chicago mob in,' said Freda.

'They'll get a surprise if they do,' said Otley. 'And we don't need machine-guns – Percy Dredger's sent for a cross-bow out of the Empire Stores catalogue.'

'We don't want any bloodshed,' Freda reminded him again.

'There's no room in the cellar; it's full of Russians,' I said.

'We'll throw 'em in the tarn with their boots full of cement,' said Tom, flicking through the Yellow Pages to see where he could get it.

'Or bury them under the Aire Valley Trunk Road,' said Otley. 'They'll never find 'em there!'

'In Sicily they wear sheepskins and have meetings in old farm houses,' I said. 'Did you see them in *The Godfather*?'

'That's only the old Moustache Petes,' said Otley. 'They wear Savile Row suits over here.'

'And wasn't it lovely music!' drooled Freda.

There were plenty of old barns and derelict farms round here, and no shortage of sheep to get skins off, so we were all right there. It was the Savile Row suits we were short of.

'They do like you to look respectable,' said Otley. 'They make short work of clowns.'

We had some cocoa and spam sandwiches with Daddy sauce, then put the box on just in time to see two frogs copulating under six inches of ice, followed by an item on sexually transmitted diseases among the koala bears.

'It's always when you're eating,' complained Otley.

Tom and Freda went home and Mike came back from playing chess with Julian. We told him about the Mafia but he said we'd forgotten something very important. Pray what was that asked Otley.

'Where are you going to get a horse's head from?' he wanted to know.

I wanted a word with him about his behaviour the other night at the Shuttle. Coming to our table and snarling at us like that! Why didn't he go and snarl at Jimmy One Eye? But he was gone. I would have to write him another letter:

'Dear Boy

It is unseemly of a fine young man with a reversible nylon body-warmer to be observed making faces at his mother. I much enjoyed your account of the workings of your friend's COMPACT DISC PLAYER WITH QUARTZ DIGITAL SYNTHESIZER STEREO TUNER, CASSETTE DECK WITH FULL LOGIC CONTROL, SPEAKERS AND RACK. But I anxiously await the answers to the many questions I have asked you. Adieu.'

I went to bed instead and looked through the keyhole on the way upstairs to see what he was doing. The light was out.

. . . . .

The next morning Kit asked us to dress up like people in a French Impressionist painting and go and sit under the umbrella outside the café. Myrtle, with her long thin legs and pink frills, looked like a flamingo, Freda looked like a Cabbage Patch doll with a silly smirk and I was an old-fashioned humbug in brown and white satin stripes.

'You sit here between them,' Kit said to Otley who looked like a barber's pole with a straw boater on.

'And you just be walking past,' he told Tom who had a string of onions round his neck.

'I hope you've got the tripe to go with 'em,' joked Tom.

'No but I've got some snails,' Kit said, putting a glass jar down on the table. Myrtle screamed and covered her face up with the daily paper.

'Don't be silly, they're dead,' he assured her.

I hoped he wouldn't come too near me as I was ready to burst into flames and it would be awkward with Otley sitting beside me.

'Keep your eyes open for the Eyeties,' he said, giving me a dig in the ribs which made me wince. How different it would have been with Kit in our little cottage. He would be strong but gentle, lifting me up and laughing with joy when our golden-haired brood brought home their Sunday School prizes to show us.

'You pour out the Pernod,' Kit directed like Cecil B. de Mille.

'It tastes like aniseed balls,' said Freda grimacing.

Kit sketched in the outlines and indicated the colours

then said he would finish it indoors. I helped him with his easel as the rest made their way into the café. I couldn't stay, I told him.

'I'd like to paint you again,' he said. 'The Queen of Hearts making the tarts – not stealing them.'

'I've paid for my crime,' I said. 'Will society never let me forget it?'

'No!' he said.

When I joined the others for a coffee there were two dark strangers occupying a corner table and the atmosphere was strained.

'We're going to be massacred,' whispered Freda when I went to help her in the kitchen. They measured us up with appraising looks as they ate their ham and eggs, dabbing at their mouths with a napkin. Then the taller of the two bent to say something in the other's ear. The fat one nodded and came towards us slowly like oozing sludge.

'My God! what's he going to do?' said Freda.

'Where's Otley?' I asked. 'He's never here when he's wanted.'

'He went off up the road after a Japanese,' she wailed.

I stood paralysed as he placed his hands on the counter and raised his eyebrows at me.

'I didn't do it,' I said trembling. 'I don't know anything about it.'

'*Scusi*,' he said in high falsetto, 'you gotta da tomato sauce?'

I looked under the counter and was relieved to find a plastic bottle shaped like a tomato. I handed it to him.

'*Grazie*,' he said, holding it as if it were a dead rat.

I gave them some toast and marmalade and collected the dirty plates, straining my ears at the fractured English.

'Ifa da boss givesa da okay we starta shooting nexta week.'

They had their heads close together when I took them some fresh coffee and toast. I bent down to scratch my ankle so that I could hear them better.

'Ifa da bossa finds outa,' the tall one said, drawing a hand across his throat and making a noise like a bacon-slicer.

'God help us!' said Freda. 'I'm going to dial 999!'

'They're coming!' I said, panic-stricken as they advanced.

The tall one fingered his tie and turned his dark glasses on us.

'You hava da rooma?' he inquired.

'*Si si*,' I told him. '*Molto bene* room.'

'I didn't know you spoke Italian,' said Freda in amazement.

'Where ara da bambinos?' he wanted to know, looking all around.

'This my bambino,' said Freda as Julian came in smart as paint, with his blazer buttoned up and his school cap on. 'Say something,' she told him behind her hand as he gave the Italians stare for stare.

'In two hundred and fifty million years,' he announced, 'the sun will have turned into a red giant.'

IT WAS reported to us that Carlo and Luigi had been heard asking Mr Grimshaw if he could have an outsize coffin ready in two weeks. Aunt Janey saw them in the cemetery and Granny Blinks heard them outside her shop saying the old Mill House would be just right for a brothel as it had a sleazy, run-down look.

'Well it's not doing much as a museum,' I joked, but nobody laughed. Myrtle swooned over Luigi and said he could put her in a bordello any time. Otley quickly put her in her place.

'We'll see what Billy has to say about that,' he scolded. 'You said no more foreigners.'

'The heart has its reasons,' she said, throwing out Billy's snapdragons and replacing them with a blood-red rose. 'And we're invited to dinner at their place.'

'It's a trap,' said Otley, kicking my patchwork tortoise. 'But I'll go anyway just for curiosity.'

That night Percy Dredger rang to say he thought he'd seen Carlo and Luigi heading for the open moor so we piled into the car and went for a midnight picnic. The three-quarter moon lay on the wooded hills like a rugby ball kicked into touch, and after going up and down and round and round with not an Italian in sight we stopped to eat our sandwiches. You can't see what you're eating in the dark Otley complained, examining the contents of his sandwich closely.

'It's salmon and cucumber,' I told him.

'I don't want botulism,' he said.

'Would you like an individual fruit pie then?'

'No, it's like eating dusty old shoe-boxes.'

'Well I don't think them Eyeties are up here,' said Freda. 'There's not a soul about.'

'What would they come up here for anyway?' observed Tom.

'Looking for an old farmhouse,' said Otley.

'Or a sheepskin,' I said, because Miss Armitage said it was important not to squash him and give him an inferiority complex.

We sat in silence while Otley studied the moon through his binoculars and then he put them away and leapt to his feet.

'I'm going for a swim,' he said taking off his shirt. 'I'm not sitting here like an old folks' home.'

'And me,' said Tom, going behind the car to undress.

'We've got no costumes,' Freda said.

'Go without,' said Otley. 'God made swimming before he made costumes.' Soon we were naked like four misshapen Adams and Eves.

My cares melted away as the soft, peaty water slipped over my shoulders like a silk chemise. Otley went through the water like the Loch Ness monster sending a tidal wave slapping up the bank. I floated on my back looking up at the stars. It was almost like old times. When we got out there were two policemen in a patrol car waiting for us; it seemed they were not very pleased.

'Playin' at water-babies are we?'

We stood in a row holding our hands in front of us, like footballers waiting for a penalty kick.

'Sorry Officer,' I lied. 'Would you like a sandwich?'

'And this is Mrs Doasyouwouldbedoneby is it?' he asked.

'No, it's Mrs Craven.'

'Swimmin' in reservoirs is not allowed,' he told us.

'We used to go in the big dam when we were kids,' said Tom.

'They allow sailing in it don't they?' said Otley aggrieved.

'Boats has a cleaner bottom than yours,' said the law enforcer. 'We have to drink that when you lot have done muckin' about in it.'

'You mean we get it straight out of here?' said Tom. 'No wonder I've always got belly-ache.'

They let us go home after promising not to do it again and Otley gave them some friendly advice.

'Keep your eyes open,' he told them. 'There's Japs and Eyeties roaming about up there somewhere.'

The next day Tom and Freda felt it necessary to have a quiet word with me about recent events. They were going to put their foot down even if they were fond of old Otley. Enough was enough.

'We can't let a lunatic run our lives,' said Tom reasonably.

'No,' said Freda. 'We might as well have a screw loose ourselves.'

• • • • •

This is nice I thought as Carlo sat us round the pine table and poured out glasses of Asti Spumante.

'Mind he hasn't slipped you a Mickey Finn,' said Otley.

We had chunks of crusty bread and hot, buttery pasta with garlic sauce and Parmesan, served on thick earthenware platters.

'Ees good,' said Luigi from behind his dark glasses.

'*Molto bene*,' I said, eating a fig with my coffee, and getting a kick on the shins from Otley.

Myrtle looked good too in her emerald silk with a bandeau to match. Her hair, washed with henna, streamed like molten lava down her back. I wore my barn-dancing frock with the red poppies in case I got doused with tomato sauce, but I needn't have bothered.

Luigi picked his teeth with a handmade toothpick as Carlo poured out more wine. Yes, he told Myrtle, he had fallen madly in love with her at first sight, she was just like his Mamma.

Carlo looked uneasy. His black eyes narrowed under their puffy lids, his fat fingers slid into his hip pocket and his fleshy lips opened and shut like a grouper about to devour its prey. Everything they said in reply to Otley's questioning went to confirm his suspicions. The boss lived in Calabria, he liked the seclusion of the mountains. City life was not for him although he owned pizza parlours in London and New York not to mention a casino or two. He was Carlo's mother's cousin and Luigi's uncle – they liked to keep the business in the family, and they were here to see if Low Riding was suitable for taking over.

'How does he pay you?' Otley wanted to know for some reason.

'A percentage ofa da take,' said Luigi.

'And if you playa da ball ees something fora you,' said Carlo.

Myrtle was on her fifth drink and capsizing towards Luigi.

'Can you find me a job?' she asked, looking into his glasses.

'We alwaysa wanta woman,' he assured her.

'I've had enough of this,' said Otley, jumping up from the table. He swaggered across the room, like they do in the Westerns when they say 'Who's ramroddin' this outfit?' and whirled suddenly around with his pistol pointed at Luigi.

'I hope your insurance is paid up, hombre, because from now on you're a dead man.'

Myrtle screamed and waved her arms like a windmill.

'Not you, sit down,' said Otley.

'He's stubbed his fag out on my hair,' she said, drenching the sizzling ends with a glass of Chianti.

'What eesa theesa?' Luigi wanted to know.

'They think you're the Mafia,' she told him.

'Eesa no Mafia,' Carlo said. 'Easa cinema shoota.'

'Then what's all this about outsize coffins and turning our home into a brothel?' asked Otley, not convinced.

'That's not very nice is it?' said Freda.

Luigi dipped into a brief-case and produced a sheaf of papers which would explain everything.

'Picture shoota, no bomba shoota,' he said, passing them round.

His uncle had been a prisoner of war in Fitchet felds. It was the happiest time of his life. He had a good story to tell and the Keighley and Worth Valley steam trains would come in handy. A sum of ten thousand pounds was suggested for the use of the café and the old house, and double time for weekends.

'It's an offer I can't refuse,' said Otley. 'But there's one other thing – why do you wear sunglasses all the time?'

'Eesa pink eye,' Luigi said, taking off his glasses. 'Eesa no good.'

'Ugh!' said Myrtle.

Suddenly there was a commotion in the doorway and Billy Delph burst in with a shotgun demanding to know where Myrtle was.

'He's our leading citizen,' I explained.

Myrtle was cross-eyed and swaying from side to side like a hollyhock in the wind. Billy had got a special licence and they could be married tomorrow. Myrtle poured out another drink.

'I haven't got a trousseau, I can't get married tomorrow.'

'You asked me to buy a bloody Wimpey house,' he told her. 'Now you can bloody well come and live in it!'

Myrtle's bottom lip stuck out in defiance. It was the irresistible force meeting the immovable object and in the end the immovable object was removed by her crowning glory from our presence.

'I keep telling her to get it cut,' said Freda.

'That Luigi,' said Otley when we got home. 'Eesa nicea chap.'

He had not enjoyed himself as much for a long time. He could cope with swash and buckle any day of the week – it was grinding domesticity he couldn't stand. Had he emptied his waste paper basket this week? Would he mind fetching a cabbage out of the allotment? And pop into the Co-op on the way back for a packet of Oxo cubes? It was enough to drive you mad!

'That reminds me, Miss Armitage says . . .' I began hesitantly.

'Sod Miss Armitage!' he said.

I left him watching a documentary about the Opium War and went off to bed. Was Mike in I wondered? There was no sound coming from his room, so I stopped to apply myself to the keyhole. What was that sitting on the chair? It was a bedraggled mop-head made of purple ostrich feathers! Now how did that get there? He would never tell me of course. *Omertà* – or something. I would have to write him a letter.

'Dear Boy,

> It has come to my attention that a fine young Englishman, in the heat of the moment . . .'

But what's the use. Blood is thicker than ink and he would only say Susan dropped it and next door's dog ran off with it.

I went to bed and sat by the window to drink my slippery elm. It would all be different in my little cottage with Kit: there would be no secrets, our blue-eyed angels would have told us everything without being asked: 'Is there anything else you want to know Mummy?' they would have asked before scampering off to sweep the leaves up from the garden path. Kit would have come in from his work in the fields, smelling of new-mown hay. 'Is there anything you want to know darling?' he would say, swinging me round.

THE NEXT morning I warned my son about getting impaled on Susan Mitchell's spikes, then went across to Bobbin Yard to see how the portrait was coming along. It looked something like a pile of theatrical props flung into a corner and forgotten.

'I can't do faces,' Kit told me unnecessarily.

On the mantelpiece was a photograph of three angelic children with golden curls, just like our little brood in the thatched cottage. The little darlings! And who were they I inquired.

'It's somebody I know,' he said, drawing my attention to a competition for a hundred pounds' worth of groceries every week for a year.

'I'm on a diet,' I reminded him.

'I know but you can let me have them,' he said.

We spent a pleasant hour trying to think of a reason in less than ten words why we wanted five thousand two hundred pounds' worth of food from Multimarket. All of them lies. It would be easier to tell the truth and put 'Because I'm greedy!'

We held hands and listened to some of *Carmina Burana* and then looked at pictures of Breughel's merry peasants dancing in a ring. It was heady stuff and Kit's beard came closer, scratching my left cheek like the stuffing in Granny's old horsehair sofa. It was all very well, but I had no time for an orgy.

'I've got some ironing to do,' I said jumping up quickly.

I gave him some empty Persil boxes before I went as he was saving up for an Awayday.

'If you won't come,' he said, 'I'll take somebody else.'

What could I say?

'And when he goes away next week come over one night.'

My mouth opened and shut like a goldfish and no sound came out. I wanted to say 'Yes' but something held me back.

'No need to say anything,' he went on as if he could read my thoughts. 'Just come over – whenever you feel like it.'

I fled across into the safety of my own kitchen and made some beans on toast for Otley who had been taking tickets in the museum. Only nobody had turned up.

'If nobody comes again tomorrow I'll blow the place up,' he declared in a fit of pique.

'What about the Russians in the cellar?' I asked him.

'I'd forgotten about that,' he said.

It did seem at times as if we were living down a rabbit-hole like *Alice in Wonderland*. Nobody was aware of our existence. It would all be different when filming started though. But that would present its problems. Already a petition had been handed to Luigi demanding a role for Queen Victoria if Mussolini was going to be in it.

'Eesa deada,' said Luigi.

'So is Mussolini,' he was told.

'Eesa deada longa,' he said.

Otley and I sat down with our fast food and switched on the box. Soon we were viewing a company of horse-flies demolishing what appeared to be an old Yorkshire pudding.

'What's this then?' I inquired, looking in the *Radio Times*.

'It's the natural history of a cow-pat,' he informed me.

'I don't think I want anything to eat,' I said.

Well, would I take *The Sicilians* back to the library and bring him *Shogun*, because he'd read in the paper that Mrs Thatcher was going to sell off British Water.

'She might as well sell the bloody lot of us to Japan.'

He would be taking it to Cornwall to read when the fish weren't biting. Don't drop it in the water I warned him. Had he packed his Swiss army knife? He had. Had he remembered his field-glasses? He had. And how much money would he be taking?

'Mind your own bloody business,' he said.

'He'll be all right,' said Dr Moss over the telephone. 'I'll give him some different tablets before he goes.'

And why wasn't I going with him to give him some back-up?

'He doesn't want me,' I said, feeling like the odd one out in Musical Chairs.

'That's the trouble,' he said. 'It's relations that drive us mad – still, never mind, you can't help it.'

Eventually we received a card from Tintagel saying it wasn't a bit like in *Camelot* and unless the weather picked up he would be back in time for the Ancient Britons' walk to Top Withens.

I looked across to Bobbin Yard and wondered what the poor lonely man was doing. Fretting about with his pots and pans and nobody to soothe his fevered brow. One of life's little ironies. Kit wanted me and couldn't have me. Otley had me and didn't want me. But what did Kit say the other morning? Come over any time I felt like it and don't bother to say anything. Just come. Well I might feel like it tonight, I thought, and what's more I would put Pocahontas on again and hang the consequences. Who cares!

'Please God,' I prayed, 'let the weather pick up in Tintagel.'

Myrtle was on her honeymoon in Grange-over-Sands so I couldn't ask her opinion but I knew what her answer would be. Freda I was not so sure about so I went over to help in the café.

'. . . and Sirius is only eight point six light years away,' Julian was telling the Italians as they ate.

'Eesa gooda kida,' said Luigi as he bought him a choc-ice and some jelly babies.

'Don't waste your money,' said Freda, putting Julian's cap on straight. 'He'll only line them up and throw darts at them.'

I told her my secret and she was shocked at first and then changed her mind. I had been understanding about Nancy and it was only fair – I was entitled to one last fling. She made it sound as if I was due to be executed on the morrow.

'We won't say anything,' she assured me. 'But only this once.'

'*Arrivederci*,' I said to our startled guests.

• • • • •

I waited until it was dark that evening before getting myself ready. Now I knew what Guy Fawkes must have felt like when he went to blow up the Houses of Parliament. Otley had gone to the same school as him in York, so he was almost one of the family.

I showered and applied my Tunisian Tan liberally all over just in case, put on my British Home Stores moccasins and squeezed into my buckskins. Wampum on and head-band in place. I could hardly recognize myself as I walked towards the tarnished mirror in the half-light.

'Where are you off to dressed like that?' Mike wanted to know.

'Spying,' I said with great presence of mind.

I looked out of the window to see what Kit was doing. His light was on but all was quiet. Poor soul, I expect he was dreaming of our little love-nest at the edge of the woods. We would just have come back from picking blackberries, the children would be carrying posies of wild flowers and they would all be singing and dancing round me while I made a blackberry pie.

I ran breathless into the night, colliding with two shadowy figures on the way. Were they Japanese?

'What eesa theesa?' inquired an Italian falsetto.

It was Carlo and Luigi, thank goodness! No need to send a telegram to Tintagel. I flung myself bodily at the cottage door and fell headlong into the room. Kit was there, waiting for me.

'I'm here!' I cried, holding out my arms to embrace him.

Then I became aware of strange faces regarding me with curiosity. One, two, three, four. But three of them were not so strange. Hadn't I seen them before, on a photograph?

'This is my wife Elaine,' said Kit as a cool blonde came forward to take my hand.

'This is Camilla,' she told me. 'Paul, our son and heir, and Victoria.'

A fat, rosy baby with a dimpled smile was held up for my inspection. So that's where he gets his cupids from! But what about the big fat slug he was painting the other day. It wasn't me, was it?

'This is Mrs Craven,' Kit said. 'She's in the Amateur Operatic Society – they're doing *Rose Marie* this week.'

I forced a smile and accepted a drink, patting baby on her fat golden curls. She was lovely, I said, they were very lucky.

'We call her Bluebell,' Kit explained. 'Because we got her in the bluebell woods.' Man and wife exchanged a secret smile.

I asked Kit how his painting was progressing and he said he was doing well since he had adopted a new style. Not sure what to do next, I accepted another drink.

'Did you want something?' inquired Elaine with a glacial smile like Hans Christian Anderson's Snow Queen.

'Could I borrow a cup of sugar?' I said impulsively. 'I want to make some rock buns.'

'At this time of night?' she said with eyebrows raised.

'Well, everybody's out' I said, as if it was my usual practice in such circumstances.

I grabbed the sugar and fled, stifling a sob. I made some tea and sandwiches and cried all through the ten o'clock news. My false eyelashes lay in the saucer like drowned spiders. My face became striped like park railings. I tore off my wig and flung it into the far corner of the room where it lay like a dead cat. I was still sitting there feeling sorry for myself when Mike came in and asked if there was anything he could get me. No there wasn't.

'I didn't think you'd miss dad that much,' he said.

. . . . .

Although I wanted to crawl under a stone the next day and keep the wood-lice company I forced myself to get up and do something. Anything – but what? Then I remembered I had to turn the attic out before Otley came back. I would find out once and for all the secret of the box. Arming myself with dusters, polish and vacuum cleaner, not forgetting a flask of coffee and a packet of ginger biscuits, I would stay up there for as long as it took.

There was a stuffed pike and a chest expander, old Sunday supplements and Manchester United football programmes, a Bible and a sex maniac's diary, a Samurai sword and an Isle of Lewis chess set made from a plastic mould he got from the *Exchange and Mart.* That was just the top layer. When I had finished I was careful to put everything back in the mess that I found it in, since my husband was allergic to spick and span. A break for coffee and then, bracing myself for the nasty shock I was about to receive, I opened the box.

I extracted the house deeds and insurance policies, then a lump came into my throat at the sight of blue speckled birds' eggs carefully wrapped in cotton-wool, and a fading photograph taken on our honeymoon when he was the laughing golden boy. At the bottom were his army things. A red beret and a Pegasus arm flash, an oak leaf on the red, white and blue ribbon of the War Medal. What did that mean? Mentioned in dispatches it seemed. The words leapt off the page at me – exemplary soldier – with no thought for his own safety – an inspiration to all – recommending Corporal Craven. Memories came flooding back and I fought back the tears. But why the secrecy?

I heard the door slam which meant that Mike was back home from school and I called him in.

'Sit down,' I told him. 'I don't know how you're going to take this.'

'Tell me the worst,' he said, eyeing the displaced floorboards, 'whatever it is I have a right to know.'

'Your father,' I said, 'was a blooming hero!'

Mike inspected the contents of the metal box for himself and casually replaced them.

'Good old dad,' he said and went off to practise his guitar.

Ungrateful brat, I thought, that's all he's good for.

WHEN I went over to help Freda with the washing-up, Kit was just setting off with his easel. I was about to toss my head and walk straight past him, but if I did he might think I was annoyed about something. Why should I worry about him anyway when my husband was a hero? I put on a Mona Lisa expression.

'I'm sorry about the other night,' he said, dropping his box of paints on the cobbles. I even picked them up for him.

'I hope they're all right,' he said. 'They cost me ten pounds seventy-five pence without the brushes.'

'How are the little kiddiewinks?' I asked him.

'You should have let me know,' he told me sheepishly.

'You said I could come over any time,' I reminded him.

'I know but I didn't think you would,' he said.

He hoped it wouldn't make any difference to my feelings

for him. He still felt the same way about me, he said, looking at me like a spaniel waiting for his chocolate drops.

'Look, I don't want to get involved with other people's wives and children,' I had to say. 'I've enough with my own relations.'

'So it's a toy-boy you want is it?'

'Yes,' I said. It sounded like a good idea.

I said I'd still save my Persil boxes for him and I hoped he enjoyed his Awayday. They were going to the Garden Festival at Liverpool.

'We can still be friends then?' he wanted to know. I resisted the temptation to pull his toe-nails out one by one.

'Why not?' I said with a toss of my curls.

We slapped hands on the deal like gypsies at a horse fair and went our separate ways.

• • • • •

'. . . and one day,' Julian was telling Carlo and Luigi, 'the earth might be devoured by a black hole.'

'Oh dear!' said Freda. 'I hope not.'

How did I get on the other night, had I enjoyed myself? She hoped I'd made the best of it because I must never do it again.

'Do what?' asked Julian.

'Go to bed without cleaning her teeth,' his mother told him.

'I had a great time,' I said. 'Met his charming wife and family and we are all bosom pals now.'

'I didn't know he was married,' said Freda.

'Oh yes! I knew right from the start,' I lied.

Carlo and Luigi finished their ham and eggs and bought Julian a Wall's Cornetto before they went. Carlo opened his mouth wide. Was he going to sing it? No he wasn't, he was only yawning.

'Theesa fooda,' he said, 'eesa why Inglesi kissa lika plumma pudding.'

'Eesa maka joka,' said Luigi as they left to go cinema shoota.

'*Arrivederci*,' I called after them.

We amused ourselves for an hour or two polishing floors and emptying the pigswill into a bin for Stalin to collect. Then we scrubbed up after depositing our rubber gloves in the sink like the brain surgeons in *Your Life in Their Hands*, and sat down to a well-earned break.

'Isn't that Otley?' asked Freda pointing to a weary figure laden with canvas bags, fishing-rods, and holdalls trudging up the road. My hero had come home to escort me on the walk to Top Withens as threatened. It was early closing tomorrow so Tom and Freda would be coming as well if she could drag him away from his cabbages.

Otley had travelled all night and was ready for bed. He put our presents in a heap on the table and told us to help ourselves. There was a plate of rock fish fingers and chips, a bucket and spade, a mug with King Arthur on it, a miniature treasure chest with chocolate money and a flag with a skull and cross-bones.

'I'd have brought you a shark-skin purse,' he told me, 'but then you've got no money, have you?' I searched my handbag to find out.

'No,' I said. 'I've only got four pence.'

. . . . .

We met the Ancient Britons the next day at one o'clock. Our leader counted us several times before he came to a decision as we were milling around in an ever-changing shape.

'Stand still a minute,' he called. 'I've got to get it right in case we lose anybody.'

Eventually he thought there were thirty-six of us but there was an invisible man yet to put in an appearance.

'Mr Birkinshaw's just gone to the Post Office for a stamp.'

He came out licking his stamp, stuck it on a postcard and pushed it into the letter-box, and we were ready to move off. Up past the Brontë Parsonage, squash through the stile and take the path across the field.

'"A little and a lone green lane,"' somebody recited.

'What?' asked Mr Birkinshaw.

'It's one of Emily's poems,' we told him.

'Oh aye!' he said.

'Ignorant git,' muttered Otley.

Through another stile which took us back on to the road. Why had we gone all that way round the field when we could have stayed on the road in the first place?

'I thought it would be more interesting for you,' our leader said. 'It's boring walking on the road.'

'It was boring in that field,' said Otley with his mouth shut.

We followed the road round Penistone Hill and on to the path leading to the Brontë Falls.

'Can you slow up a bit?' came a voice from the rear. 'Miss Cartwright's got a bad leg.'

'I don't know what's the matter with it,' she apologized. 'It was all right when I got up this morning.'

'Silly thing to do,' said her friend. 'Coming out with your leg.'

When we reached the Brontë Chair, Miss Cartwright thankfully sat down on it and then decided to call it a day. The rest of us crossed Sladen Beck on the old clapper bridge and toiled up the steep hillside. At the top was a patch of bilberries so we stopped to snatch a few. We might get enough for a saucer pie.

'Watch your sticks in this mud,' our leader called. 'It pulls the rubber ends off.'

'My back aches,' Eddie Umpleby complained. 'I didn't realize it was so far – I thought it was just behind the parsonage.'

'Well if you want to go back I'll go with you,' Mr Birkinshaw volunteered. 'It's not safe to be on your own these days.'

'Good riddance to bad rubbish,' said Otley.

The views were magnificent but we had no time to enjoy them as our leader was striding out well in front. How did he expect us to keep up with him with his big feet and long legs? He walked from one end of the Himalayas to the other for his holidays last year. I mean ter say! When we passed a derelict house and met the Pennine Way coming down a few of our number decided to go with it.

'You can take a short cut if you like and follow the Pennine Way down to Ponden Hall,' he called after their disappearing bobble-hats

'When are we going to have our sandwiches?' a weak voice asked.

We were nearly there now and you could just about see Top Withens. It was that dark smudge on the horizon, half hidden in a dip. Our eyes raked the skyline. Now you see it, now you don't.

'Take care not to damage the walls,' our leader called. I looked at my grazed knuckles and wondered what he meant.

'And always close the gates behind you,' he went on. I looked for a gate but couldn't find one.

'Over the moors is Wycoller; the ruined hall is Ferndean Manor in *Jane Eyre* – it's in Lancashire though,' he said, savagely kicking at a boulder. I was still looking for *Wuthering Heights*.

By the time we got there I had a splitting headache and was too tired to eat my sandwiches but I enjoyed my tea and aspirins. The sheep gathered round us in a circle as if a black magic ritual was about to commence.

'Don't look at them,' said Ernie, 'and they'll go away.'

The ruined farmhouse had been cemented down by the council to stop souvenir hunters from making away with it entirely. They got there just in time and a plaque had been put on the wall. Among other things it told us that 'the buildings, even when complete, bore no resemblance to the house she described'. I was glad that Otley was here to share my disappointment.

'Can I have your sandwiches?' he asked, delving into my rucksack. 'Plenty of hiding places round here for them.'

'For who?' I said absent-mindedly.

'Them,' he said mysteriously.

I wanted to ask him about the army but thought it better to wait for a more intimate moment, like when he wanted some clean pyjamas, or a new string vest. The quiet was therapeutic.

After a while the sheep decided we were a dull lot and went off to do more exciting things like getting stuck on the barbed-wire. We were able to enjoy a wool-free view.

'When you're ready,' called our leader putting on his pack.

Going back was easier and we chattered like a pack of monkeys all the way. All except Otley.

'Did you enjoy your holiday then?' we wanted to know.

'No,' he said.

'Sorry about that,' said Freda, tutting in sympathy.

'That's all right, I never do,' he said frankly.

'Why do you go then?' inquired Tom reasonably.

'It makes a change from not enjoying myself here,' said Otley.

Presently we found a gate to remember to shut behind us

and then lacerated ourselves on more walls in an effort not to damage them.

'This is Yorkshire Water Board property,' Ernie Briggs told us. 'So treat it with respect.'

'I don't know what they do with it, it's not fit to drink these days,' said a shocked Ancient Briton in a loud voice.

We looked the other way in confusion. Did they know about us swimming in it? What were they hinting at? Had somebody blabbed?

'It's the peat,' Otley told them. 'It gets everywhere.'

'And it's good for the complexion,' I said. 'Soft and silky.'

'If I want a suntan I'll go to Majorca,' said the voice.

'Are we all here?' Ernie called, doing some mental arithmetic.

Ten had fallen by the wayside so there should be twenty-seven but try as we may we could only make it twenty-six.

'We've lost somebody,' he cried, eliminating us one by one on his fingers. 'Mrs Schofield, Arnie Earnshaw, Oggie Butterfield and their Sammy, Frances and Edie, Jack Wintersgill . . .'

'It's Amy Lightowler!' a triumphant cry went up. 'She nipped off down the clough, her Marlene lives down there.'

'As long as we know,' he said.

We reached Haworth and clung exhausted round the bus stop.

'We've just missed the six o'clock bus,' Ernie announced. 'We've got thirty minutes' wait for the next one. I'm off down the gully.' Did we want to join him? No we didn't so he went off down the road towards the gully alone. A brave sight in his flapping gaiters.

'It's all right for him,' said Freda. 'He's got long legs.'

'I've lived here all my life,' said Otley, 'and I've never seen Wuthering Heights before.'

'What did you think of it then?' we asked.

'Not much,' he said, 'there's no conveniences.'

While we waited at the bus stop a young Japanese girl came up to us and asked where 'Heathcriff rived'. We pointed it out on the map and said it was a long way. She wanted to see it before she caught the late train from Reeds to Rondon.

'They're think we're stupid,' said Otley later on the bus. 'All that way from Japan by herself. What's she up to?'

I had read that *Wuthering Heights* was their favourite novel. They liked the fierce passions and the delicate wild-flowers on the heath. It touched the Japanese soul – like cherry blossom and hara-kiri. If I believed that I'd believe anything, Otley said.

'Why do you think they've come over here with their microchips?' he asked us looking through his field-glasses. 'It's not because they like the flora and fauna.

Low Riding went about its business in the twilight. Stalin was saying good night to his pigs and Granny Blinks was running up the road to post her football coupon. Kit, I thought ruefully, would be sharing our love-nest with another; our little angels would be dancing round her and asking if there was anything she wanted to know. Would Otley have a word with Mike some time?

'What about?' he asked in amazement.

• • • • •

We had some fast food when we got in, then I went upstairs to have a shower and change into something 'more comfortable' for the evening. I was too tired to bother with a candle-lit dinner but a television meal with the reading lamp on might be just as good. Where was Mike? His keyhole was stuffed up with Kleenex tissues – it gave me quite a shock.

Otley was examining the ad column in the local paper to see what he could sell. He didn't feel ready for work yet.

'Have we any scrap gold, Victorian christening gowns, or baby grands?' he inquired.

'No,' I had to say.

'Any French dolls with bisque faces?'

'No,' I said, feeling a dismal failure.

'Have we got anything we can sell?' he asked irritably.

'There's that old gas oven,' I said. 'They buy them and do them up. And an old sheepskin coat – some poor soul might like it.'

'I want that myself,' he said.

'I've been thinking,' I said, pouring him a stiff drink. 'Why have you kept it a secret all these years what you did in the army?' I knocked one back myself and nearly choked on it.

'How do you mean?' he asked.

'We have a right to know, me and Mike, your nearest and dearest.'

'Give over,' he said, going back to the newspaper.

'It's nothing to be ashamed of,' I blurted out.

'What isn't?'

'The oak leaf – for bravery.'

'Have you been spying on me?' he demanded.

'It's in the blood,' I said.

'That's the last time I'll let you clean my room out,' he said. 'I can't find where anything is.'

'Why don't you tell us about it, get it off your chest?'

'Because I was a bloody idiot, catch me doing it again!'

'You're too old now anyway,' I assured him.

'Good job too!'

'Mike knows everything,' I said fearfully.

'I didn't want to set him a bad example,' he explained.

'You've got to look after Number One – if you don't nobody else will.'

I busied myself in the kitchen for a while to let him calm down and hid the oven gloves out of the way in case he came in. The Man in the Moon peeped in through the window and he seemed to be smiling. It was funny the way things worked out. All this aggravation, and all I ever wanted was a little cottage with roses round the door – somewhere peaceful out in the countryside.

'You'll get that when you're dead,' Otley always said.

I carried the trays into the sitting-room and put one beside our hero's chair. Miss Armitage wanted to see him this week, I told him casually. She was concerned about his welfare.

'She wants her head examining,' he said. 'Worrying about the likes of me.'

The door slammed and to my astonishment Mike appeared all smiles. Was it somebody's birthday?

'Hello Dad,' he said cheerfully as he elbowed me out of the way.

No, he said, he wasn't going out tonight. He'd stay in and watch some television with us for a change. Besides, Susan had to wash the spikes out of her hair as Luigi had given her a part in his film. She was to play Connie, the dairy maid who had hidden Luigi's uncle in a haystack when the Home Guard were searching for escaped prisoners of war.

I picked up my crossword puzzle with a contented sigh. This was IT, we were a nuclear family at last! There was Daddy Bear, Mummy Bear and little Baby Bear.

'I'll go and make some tea,' I said, dropping my crossword on the floor in my excitement.

'I'll do it,' said Mike, charging past me into the kitchen.

If this wasn't my birthday then it ought to be!

Presently he emerged with just one cup of tea and in my

innocence I held out my hand to take it, but he passed by as if I were invisible and handed it to Otley.

'Here you are Dad,' he said. 'Have you had your tablets?'

'What tablets?' asked Otley, getting up to switch on the box.

And we were just in time to see two pygmy hippos copulating in a bog, and a herd of rutting wildebeeste milling about like football hooligans. Suddenly my throat went dry and I found it difficult to swallow.

'I think I'll go to bed and read,' I told them. 'I don't want anything to eat.'